"On the way back to our apartment, I stopped at Burger Chef. I dreaded having to tell Vanessa what had happened. She'd never let me hear the end of it. The familiar smell of french fries and hamburger on the griddle was just what I'd been craving; yet the odor made me nauseous all over again. My mouth wanted food but my stomach didn't. Still, I ordered two double cheeseburgers to go. I snuck up to my rooftop hideaway and nursed my sorrows with processed cheese and a gooey hamburger on a sesame-seed bun."

JAN GREENBERG is the author of the *The Iceberg and Its Shadow* and *A Season In-Between*. Ms. Greenberg lives in St. Louis.

THE
PIG-OUT
BLUES

Jan Greenberg

LAUREL-LEAF BOOKS bring together under a single imprint outstanding works of fiction and nonfiction particularly suitable for young adult readers, both in and out of the classroom Charles. F. Reasoner, Professor Emeritus of Children's Literature and Reading, New York University, is consultant to this series.

Published by
Dell Publishing Co., Inc.
1 Dag Hammarskjold Plaza
New York, New York 10017

Laurel-Leaf Library ® TM 766734, Dell Publishing Co., Inc.

ISBN: 0-440-96977-8

RL: 7.6

Reprinted by arrangement with Farrar, Straus & Giroux, Inc.

Printed in the United States of America

April 1985

10 9 8 7 6 5 4 3

WFH

For Sandy, Joellen,
Lilly, and Kristen
with love

The Pig-Out Blues

I

"JODIE Firestone, your arms are as thick as tree trunks," my mother said on her way to the icebox. Her idea of a snack is raw cucumber with lemon juice and parsley. As I hunched over the kitchen table, cramming for a history exam, she stood glaring.

"Perfect time to comment about my weight," I snapped, "right in the middle of mid-terms. I can't concentrate any more."

One snide remark from her made two hours of memorizing my notes on the French Revolution an exercise in futility. Now all I can remember is Marie Antoinette's solution to the problem of starving peasants: "Let them eat cake!"

As soon as Mother returned to the television, I headed for the cake platter and devoured three doughnuts. Then on to Doritos, half a jar of peanut butter, and a bagel sandwich. Heated twenty seconds in the microwave, the bagel emerged hot and sort of rubbery. After smothering it with cream cheese, I added salami and a slice of onion. A masterpiece!

Back at the table, I munched on a Milky Way, swishing the chocolate filling around with my tongue. I read in

Newsweek that children who eat too much junk food exhibit excessive signs of hyperactivity. But all I want to do now is go to bed—just burrow under my blanket like a groundhog and hibernate until exams are over.

"No one would describe you as an overachiever," my mother once observed. Other evaluations of my academic performance, although less candid, coincide. "Jodie's spelling and grammar are unique," the English teacher wrote diplomatically on my last progress report. "Yet she's an avid participant in class discussions."

If talking were a course, I would get an A. Otherwise the subjects I endure at Hamilton High are simply a means to an end. If I don't show for history class, turn in science papers, and take math tests, I can't participate in extracurricular activities, and the one essential activity in my life is Mr. Wuensche's Drama Guild. Ever since I played the wicked queen in Miss Gilda Garvey's production of *Snow White*, I've wanted to be an actress. I was seven. Miss Gilda raved about my natural ability, which convinced Mother to pay another fifty dollars for lessons, a decision she has regretted ever since.

"Jodie resorts to melodrama whenever she doesn't get her way."

True. I can simulate tears, trembling, and tantrums—usually to no avail. For this reason, Drama Guild is a great outlet. There I am transformed from a teenage tubby into Ophelia or Desdemona. Mr. Wuensche (rhymes with *clinchy*) centers all our dramatic attempts around Shakespeare's comedies and tragedies. I prefer the tragedies. Long pauses, soulful eye rolling, and moaning are easy for me to project these days. It's not only that I live in the hinterlands of Connecticut or that I'm fifteen, overweight, broke, and bored; but also that I share this penthouse (a third-floor walk-up) with Vanessa Firestone, the Medusa of Main Street.

Slamming my book shut, I turned off the lights and retreated to my bedroom—the only room in our apartment with a naked light bulb hanging from the ceiling, a broken radiator, and a window facing a brick wall. The way I can tell what season it is from my room is by the temperature, stifling in the summer and freezing in the winter. I am not Cinderella, nor is Vanessa my stepmother. So why am I stuck in this dingy cell with a family of mice for companions? The answer, according to my mother, is economically based.

"This is the best place I can afford, and if you want to fix up your room, you're old enough to earn money to do it yourself."

At fifteen, with no transportation, the only place for me to work is as a car hop at Steak and Shake or dishing out ice cream at Velvet Freeze. But Vanessa considers this kind of job inappropriate for a girl with a weakness for hamburgers and french fries. So my room stays threadbare and my mother keeps after me to find suitable employment. Mother's motto is "Less is more," but she carries it to extremes.

I have few recollections of my early childhood. The photograph of a wide-eyed three-year-old in patent-leather Mary Janes and pigtails, crumpled in Vanessa's nightstand drawer, is proof that the child Jodie Firestone existed. But if I went to birthday parties, ice skating, or to the zoo, if I played all those common little-girl games, I cannot remember.

What I do remember is moving from place to place with

Vanessa, as if we were fugitives, keeping a wary distance from other people. Vanessa is definitely not the cookies-for-the-whole-neighborhood type.

Sometimes I have visions of a cheery house with a glowing fireplace and a large man smelling of pipe tobacco and reaching out to hold me. But that's a fantasy. My father was killed in Vietnam. Maybe his parachute didn't open or he stepped on a land mine. My mother must have told me once, but now I've forgotten and I'm afraid to ask. When I was younger, I made up stories that ended with his coming home. It was a way of pretending his absence was only temporary, that one day he would come bursting through the door and everything would be normal again. Whenever Vanessa mentions him, it's only to complain about "how hard it is to raise a kid without help." After a while I gave up thinking about him. There's no point in holding on to the past. But the present's not so appealing either, especially in a dark bedroom with a broken radiator.

It was so cold there, I was shivering. My breath rose like puffs of smoke. To avoid looking at my body, I pulled my nightgown over my clothes; then I undressed quickly and slid under the covers. My thoughts collided like Dodg'em cars in an amusement park. My cold hands clenched, I sat up in bed and practiced an improvisation that Mr. Wuensche taught me. If I envision a warm place, I can raise the temperature, go from Iceland to Florida through sheer force of imagination.

So I imagined a sunny place and pretty soon moved on to my favorite fantasy: becoming rich and famous. If I were rich, I could buy Mother a condominium in Miami Beach and ship her off permanently. I can picture her there: bony and tan in the Florida sun, surrounded by rich widowers in Hawaiian shirts. "I have a fat daughter," she announces, "but she's rich and famous."

Without Vanessa, I could move in with my best friend, Heather Simms, and be free of the nagging, the shrieking harangues, that alternate with disapproving silence. Occasionally her silent periods last several days and give me a chance to come and go as I please and eat TV dinners in my room. A perfect excuse for avoiding her. On rare occasions, Vanessa and I get along, but that's always based on my performance level, mainly improving my grades or losing weight.

I know I'm not the only person who has problems with her mother. *Seventeen* has a story on this dilemma in every issue. Last month a girl from Akron, Ohio, wrote: "My mother's a real pest. Whenever I turn around she's watching me, asking nosy questions." A self-help article followed, entitled "Ten Ways to Weather the Storm." It was filled with nautical expressions, advising teenagers to buffet the waves and keep their heads above water. They compared girls and their mothers to fish swimming in troubled waters. "Don't swim against the stream," they warned, "or you'll end up adrift on an endless sea." I ended up stuffing the magazine in a drawer already overflowing with helpful hints left by my mother. Most of them have to do with diet and exercise. Vanessa's a dedicated magazine subscriber, who clips these articles, along with photos of lithe ballerinas and models, and dumps them on my unmade bed every day. There's a picture of Cheryl Tiegs stuck on the refrigerator door, as well as a rearview photo of an enormous fatty pigging out in the icebox. A gentle reminder NOT TO EAT HER OUT OF HOUSE AND HOME.

No wonder I want to live with the Simmses. Not only

do they have an open-door policy on the icebox, but Heather's mother never criticizes me. She's really wonderful. Once she looked at me and said, "What a beautiful, sultry voice you have, Jodie." That felt so good I had to squeeze my eyes shut to keep back the tears. She adopted me on the spot, and their house has been my refuge ever since.

There are times when I feel sorry for Vanessa. Often she's so tired after a long day at Trumbells, where she is a buyer of ladies' garments, that she falls asleep with the "Tonight" show blaring. Tiptoeing into her bedroom to turn off Johnny Carson, I've observed her. Rumpled clothes, hair askew, caved into the chair, she sighs in her sleep. She looks so sad that I'm tempted to stroke her hair and tell her not to worry. But if she's lonely, she never admits it. Once, bumping into the door, I startled her out of a deep sleep.

"Don't stare at me," she rasped in an unsteady voice, as if she felt ashamed to be discovered at a weak moment. I'm self-conscious, too, if I catch Vanessa watching me, especially when she knits her brows and glowers, silently accusing me of being too fat.

Being fat doesn't thrill me either. But for thirteen years I was a stringbean—all legs and arms. The tallest girl in the whole elementary school. They used to put me in the back row for every class picture. I always marched last in line for school pageants. My mother bragged that I could eat and eat, but never gain weight. "Jodie's got a hollow leg." But unexpectedly I stopped growing taller. All my friends shot up; I stayed five feet. My eating habits didn't change. Instead of growing vertically, I grew horizontally. Now I don't know if my breasts are real or just fat rolls.

But I'm definitely not obese. Wanda Sue Weatherly is obese. She looks like a freak, an elephant woman, the fat lady in the circus. Me—I'm what you call pleasantly plump, full-faced, waistless, and hippy. At fifteen, that's a definite disadvantage. Chubby babies are considered cute, but not short, chunky teenagers. No one wants to pinch my cheeks or gurgle at me. I could be dressed like a *Vogue* model, but who would notice? It's hard for a person who once hated being tall to get her wish to be short, and hate that, too.

Once I was in a play called *The Monkey's Paw*. A farmer wishes for a lot of money. His wish is granted: an insurance check arrives, compensation for his only son's death. The moral: never wish on a monkey's paw. Never wish. Fantasies are okay, but don't rely on magic. Magic! Maybe that's why I love the theater. In the world of costumes and scenery, footlights and greasepaint, I can create my own magic, use my "sultry voice" and escape into places where reality ends and dreams begin. Instead of losing consciousness and taking my chances on having a nightmare, I'm awake, in control, my own invention.

Squirming under the quilts, I practiced being Lady Macbeth. "Out, damned spot," I whispered, wringing my hands for dramatic effect—and to keep warm.

2

ONE of the main reasons I love acting is that I can use someone else's words, keeping my thoughts protected, fenced in, lest they come charging forth like an angry bull. But that's only possible one afternoon a week in Drama Guild.

Right now I'm sitting in the library making a last-ditch attempt to study, to piece together the facts leading to Marie Antoinette's fateful date with the guillotine. I can picture her in satins and lace pacing around the dungeon, cursing the masses, checking her makeup for her final public appearance. That's the trouble with my studying, I always create a scenario instead of memorizing details.

Mrs. Drabble, the librarian, hovered nearby, so Heather passed a piece of gum under the table.

"I figure you need this," she said, "since you've just chewed the eraser off your pencil."

When I popped a huge bubble, the rest of the kids giggled. Drabble swung around but didn't catch me.

"You're asking for trouble," said Heather. "I suggest you concentrate your energies on the French Revolution instead of starting your own." What I love about Heather is the sense of humor she exhibits at odd moments. No one but me would suspect she's thinking funny thoughts, she looks so wide-eyed and sweet. But whenever Heather narrows those big blue eyes, I can tell she's about to make a witty remark. We became friends one afternoon at Trumbells, where we spent hours running down the up escalators. There we found our imaginations ran in funny directions too.

"Do you think I can use cue cards during the exam?" I asked. Heather's never worried about exams because she's always prepared.

"My father says the main point to remember about the French Revolution is the total inability of the monarchy to deal with the liberal and democratic forces of its age." I nodded dumbly while she continued. "In honor of the French Revolution, Mother served a gourmet meal last night: escargots, chicken Parisienne, croissants, and pâtisseries framboises. I even drank a glass of red wine. Dad discussed eighteenth-century France through three courses."

"Probably in French," I muttered, popping another large bubble. "With that dinner, I take it you're on the side of the aristocrats."

Laughing, Heather clunked me on the head with a book. "Even revolutionaries enjoy eating well."

"Are you referring to me?" Heather's one of the few people I can joke with about my weight problem.

"Never. I'm talking about my parents, who believe that a good meal stimulates conversation."

The Simmses are the kind of parents who always encourage their children. Mr. Simms took a refresher course in geometry and reads all of Heather's textbooks. When

Heather and I were studying American Indians last year, the whole family built a tepee out of canvas and wood in the front yard and held a council fire. We roasted corn, chanted, and did a sun dance. Mr. Simms, dressed in a full headdress of eagle feathers, recited Chief Black Hawk's last speech to his tribesmen. With his gaunt features, prominent nose, and resonant voice, he became Black Hawk, noble and proud, even in the face of his people's expulsion from their land. Although Mr. Simms carried on a little too long, there wasn't a dry eye in the group. The Simmses never discuss their children's report cards or question them about grades, but Heather and her brother, David, make straight A's anyway.

A pair of hands shook me roughly by the shoulders. I turned to face the looming head of the librarian.

"Do I smell Double Bubble?" she screeched.

"No, it's my cologne," I protested, swallowing the whole wad.

Mrs. Drabble has rules about gum and food in the library. Still there are cookie crumbs between the pages of books and gum stuck under the tables.

"I hear your lips flapping, missy," she said. "You'd better watch it or I'll send you down to Storage C." Storage C is the Lost and Found. Storage A is detention, but she always mixes them up.

"Storage C?" I peered at Drabble. "I'm not missing anything." This produced muffled guffaws throughout the room. Teasing Mrs. Drabble is always good for a laugh, but it's also a way of avoiding my history notes. Not so funny—especially when zero hour's in three minutes. Maybe if I cause a commotion, she'll send me to the principal's office and I'll be able to miss the history exam. It won't be the first time I've been sequestered in Storage A, which is as familiar to me as my own bedroom. As a matter of fact, both rooms have the same decor—early drab. The bell rang, but for once the expression "saved by the bell" did not apply.

We shuffled into study hall. Two honor students handed out Blue Books and the exam. Four essay questions and thirty multiple-choice. The pencil slipped through my fingers. The words were a blur. My neck throbbed as I gathered courage to decipher the questions. Even when I know the answers, I always flub exams. I panic; my mind goes blank, a tabula rasa. Simple statements suddenly become tricky, threatening. I began by repeating to myself, "You know, you know it. You know, you know it." I sat staring at the empty page while everyone else was busy scribbling. The scratching of their pencils grated on my nerves and the hissing radiator tormented me. I was surrounded by robots in preppy clothes. All four essay questions seemed exactly the same, so I wrote similar answers in different words—basically blaming Marie Antoinette, who reminds me of my mother. My concluding sentence was: "You can't have your cake and eat it too." By the time I'd muddled through five pages of wild guesses, there were four minutes left to answer the multiple-choice. Eeny, meeny, miny, moe works just as well as anything else. My mouth was parched; my stomach rumbled; I craved a strawberry milk shake and a Milky Way. The history teacher gave me a snide look when I finally handed in my Blue Book. Looking around, I discovered I was the only student left in the room.

Another bell rang and soon one thousand students converged, shouting and shoving, dashing to the exits. Friday dismissal produces more hysteria than other afternoons.

Out came Robert Bensinger, president of Drama Guild, looking like a giraffe in the midst of a herd of buffalo. When we rehearse together, people call us Mutt and Jeff. He has an amazingly square, protruding jaw that gives him a cavernous voice box (perfect for opera) but doesn't do much for his looks. With his tall, husky body and mammoth jaw, he reminds me of Frankenstein's monster. Robert has already been accepted early admission to Yale and doesn't let any of us forget it. He thinks he's too good to be in plays with the rest of the club, so he usually sits back with Mr. Wuensche and offers uncalled-for suggestions. Whatever Wuensche says, Bensinger echoes. Yet he often picks the cast, so I have to be civil to him.

"Bensinger," I shouted over the tumult of banging lockers and shrieking students, "have you decided on a winter play yet?"

He stared back as if I were a stranger. His mouth opened in a wide, dopey grin . . . the Grand Canyon. The Yale admissions committee must have been high when it accepted him.

"Don't tell me you're planning to audition, Chubs," he said in his arrogant new Yalie tone.

"I was thinking about it," I replied softly. That nickname infuriates me. Anyone else I might slug.

"As a matter of fact, Mr. Wuensche conferred with me last night and I suggested *Romeo and Juliet*—that's the most appropriate Shakespearean play I can think of for a bunch of adolescents." Appropriate? I can't think of a worse play for "a bunch of adolescents." Too much violence and sex—too suggestive, too complex.

"I can't believe Mr. Wuensche agreed to do that play," I said, shaking my head in amazement.

"He takes my advice on everything," boasted Bensinger.

Oh, right, big mouth. You're such a pro! Once I saw the play live when the Old Vic came to New York. I borrowed money from Heather and took the train by myself all the way from High Ridge. I cried and cried. The next month was spent on the roof practicing Juliet's soliloquies. Auditioning for her part will be a cinch.

"Do you know who's trying out for Romeo or Juliet?" I asked, attempting to sound cagey. Romeo could be played by a baboon for all I cared.

"Tryouts are in four weeks," he bellowed, already striding past me down the corridor. "If you're interested, you'd better shed a few pounds." Three boys turned and gaped, laughing all the way out the door. Suddenly I felt like a toadstool. Bloated and empty, I stood in the now deserted hall and cursed Robert Bensinger. I was determined to show him, my mother, and everyone else that Jodie Caroline Firestone could do whatever she set her mind to do.

3

MOTHER and her friend Myrna Hochman were watching a rerun of the Donohue show and flipping through *Women's Wear Daily* when I got home. The rerun featured five swinging singles extolling the virtues of free love and independence. Three were fashion models and the other two women owned public-relations firms. They were beautiful and sexy and earned over $100,000 per annum. For some unknown reason, Mother and Myrna identified with these women. Myrna is the cosmetics representative for Revlon, which means she stands behind the counter at Trumbells and demonstrates how to apply lip gloss. My mother gives Myrna free advice on coordinating her wardrobe, and Myrna gives Mother free beauty-care products. The result is disastrous. Mother wears too much makeup, and Myrna sports someone else's initials all over her body. Dior, Cardin, and Calvin Klein compete for attention from her neck to her feet. At the moment, a shocking-pink blouse embroidered with small *YSL*'s wins. Six gold chains are festooned around her neck. From far away, Mother and Myrna could be sisters—except Myrna is on the hefty side.

There they were bent over *WWD* searching for luminaries, bemoaning all the parties to which they were not invited. "Look at them, just look!" Vanessa was pointing to a picture of a woman smothered in ostrich feathers dancing with a bare-chested person of questionable gender. "Viscountess de Ribes had a gala at Xenon."

"What are you so excited about?" I demanded. "You wouldn't know what to do in that decadent crowd. And why would you want to?"

"It's just that those people are out there living it up while Myrna and I work our tails off."

"And what does it get us?" wailed Myrna. "After deductions for tax, social security, and the employees' benefit fund, my paycheck barely covers the rent."

"The viscountess and her cronies are throwing another bash." Vanessa flicked the page. "My Lord. I'll bet that gown cost a thousand dollars."

"Let's see." Myrna grabbed the paper. Their irritation forgotten, they began to squeal like schoolgirls.

"You two are so weird," I muttered, but secretly I wondered if I'd have a friend to giggle with when I was their age. Myrna and Vanessa laugh over the dumbest things.

"There's Jackie O.," cried Vanessa, jiggling the paper at Myrna.

They are insatiable media freaks, star-struck, collectors of trivia. Mother claims that, before I was born, she saw President Kennedy at the tie counter at Brooks Brothers. Several weeks later he was assassinated. It was then that she started her John F. Kennedy Memorial Scrapbook, filled with pictures of Jackie, Caroline, and John John. *WWD* gives her plenty of material—to use against me.

"Look, Caroline's in Paris to study at the Louvre." (Translation: Jodie never opens a book.)

"Look, John John on a date at Regine's." (Translation: Jodie's never even been asked on a date.)

"Look, Jackie in a bikini, sunbathing on the Riviera." (Needs no translation.)

"Look." I snorted. "John John and Caroline are in the wastebasket," as I ripped an old *WWD* and pitched it.

"You could learn a few lessons from those kids," said Vanessa. "They lead interesting lives."

"They should lead interesting lives with all their money and connections," Myrna interjected.

"Why do you hold them up to me?" I shouted. "John John and Caroline Kennedy make me sick."

"They have every opportunity in the world. I can't give you that, but you could be interesting, too, if you made the most of yourself. I'm just trying to demonstrate what's out there."

"There's more 'out there' than parties, clothes, and trips," I said. "I don't want to be like them."

"Well, you never will be, young lady, the way you spend your time: eating and daydreaming."

That's not true, I protested to myself. I try. I have plans. Why can't she back off and leave me alone? What are *your* priorities, I want to shout. How important are your gold chains, your new clothes, your gossip? Where is your head? Can't you tell me anything besides what a dumb, gross person I am? But I just stared back at her and felt my shoulders slump.

Maybe she noticed the defenseless look on my face because she sighed and her voice lost some of its harsh quality. "All right, I might as well admit it. Sometimes those kids make me sick, too. They have it made. If Caroline messes up, some big shot will come along and bail her out. But, Jodie, you can't afford to make mistakes. I know I'm after you too much, but who else will be?" Her voice became insistent again as she got up and paced back and forth. I knew she wanted the best for me, but her notion of the best had nothing to do with me. Just some silly fantasy.

"These should be the most wonderful years of your life," Vanessa said sadly. "I can't get it through your head that you're going to miss out if you hold on to sloppy attitudes." Sloppy, I thought, meaning FAT. What she wants me to be is some fashion plate starved to perfection. Her idea of Perfect!

"Come on, give me a kiss, Jodie," crooned Myrna, always butting in, "and tell old Auntie Myrna about your love life."

"Love life." My mother sniffed. "With that figure?" She turned to me. "You could be so pretty if you only lost about ten pounds."

You could be pretty if . . . There's a line I've heard so often that now it stimulates an automatic response. Like Pavlov's dog, I began to salivate. A ravenous urge swept over me. Whenever Vanessa made a scathing remark, I wanted to dive into the icebox. But I had vowed to start a diet, inspired by visions of myself as Juliet on the balcony calling, "Romeo, Romeo, wherefore art thou Romeo?" Juliet is slender, beautiful . . . the new me. And suddenly my mother's support was important.

"You'll be happy to know I'm beginning a new diet," I told her. "If I make a list of low-calorie food, will you buy it for me?" For once, don't lecture me, I pleaded silently. Just concentrate on what I'm asking without the editorial statements.

"Fabulous," said Mother, perking up. "Keep to seven hundred calories a day and you'll be slim in no time. I'll supervise this project. If you lose twenty pounds, I'll take you shopping at Trumbells. The only way to lose is starve and exercise." The word *starve* sounded ominous.

"Why can't my diet be fun? The last article you accidentally on purpose left on my bed was about a spa in California where they serve three elegant meals of less than seven hundred calories: watercress sandwiches, cold salmon, fresh asparagus in lemon sauce, raspberry soufflés."

"Well, this isn't the Golden Door"—Vanessa laughed—"but if you promise not to cheat, I'll try to plan an appealing diet."

I've lost and gained back a total of about forty pounds in the last two years. Pulling her calorie-counter pamphlet, *The Health Spa Diet Book*, and an exercise manual out of the cabinet, Vanessa said, "Take these. They're my bibles." I looked at the books and back at her. She follows a regimen of jogging, sit-ups, and cottage cheese religiously. Clearly it works. She's tall and bone-thin, but big-breasted. Even if I stuffed my bra and was stretched on the rack, I could never look like her.

Taking advantage of the optimistic turn in the conversation, I announced, "I'm trying for the lead in the winter play."

"Jodie, a famous actress." Mother sighed. "I always wanted to be on stage, but I got married instead." As usual, she managed to direct the statement back to herself.

"That was a mistake," commented Myrna dryly. "Don't

tie yourself up with some man, Jodie. Do something on your own first." Then Myrna and Mother began their second-favorite conversation (after the gossip columns): lost hopes and missed opportunities. One would think that if it hadn't been for the horrible men in their lives, from fathers to husbands, boyfriends to bosses, either Myrna or Vanessa might be Viscountess de Ribes by now.

"I'm going out to get some fresh air." Leaving them griping and cooing alternately over *Women's Wear Daily*, I climbed the black metal fire escape to the roof, my favorite hideaway. Sharp gusts of wind cut through me. I folded my arms to my chest and lowered my chin to avoid the cold. Dusk . . . a pink and silver sky obscured by the murky Connecticut air. The neon signs flashed on one by one: EAT, Rainbow Grill, Shell Gas. Our building is on the main drag of High Ridge, which is set on the plateau of a wide hill. A crisscross of streets defines the commercial area, with the residential section spreading like a spider web out and down the sloping hill. Our building is on a high point in town—providing a hazy view of Heather's house, a converted barn on the other side of the woods. I imagined a light coming from the dining room where her family assembled for dinner. I could picture them folding their hands for grace.

"Evening is nigh, come bow your head; we thank Thee, Lord, for this good bread." That is the first prayer I ever learned. Mother's not religious, so we never go to church. But at the Simmses', someone is always thanking the Lord for something. I've gotten in the habit of whispering little prayers now and then, too. Mostly I pray to be thin, which seems a prerequisite for success in this world—according to magazines, television, and Vanessa Firestone. What this new diet needs, I think, is an initiation rite: first a prayer, then a long bath. A fresh start.

Looking out at the familiar geography of High Ridge, I imagined all the people in this narrow-minded town I'd tell off once I was skinny.

"Listen, Robert Bensinger," taunts the famous Jodie Firestone after signing the contract for her first television series, "how would you like a walk-on as the butler? Your voice is perfect for announcing guests."

"By the way," I'd tell my teacher Mr. Foster, handing him a drop slip, "the history of the French Revolution is useless information. There are more important things to learn."

"Close my charge, Mr. Kramer." He's the stuffy manager at Trumbells, Vanessa's boss. "Saks is the only place to shop."

A chauffeur-driven limousine pulls up to Hamilton High. A crowd gathers. "Have some free tickets to my show," the glamorous new me shouts, flipping the stubs out the window. I push the automatic window button as the entire student body scrambles for the bits of scattered paper.

The last of day's gray light deepened into slate, leaving the sky starless and empty. Made me want to dissolve into the emptiness. Getting even on the roof. What a dumb idea! What good did it do to invent empty lies? What good? Furious with myself and everyone else, I kicked the wall as tears started rolling down my cheeks.

4

STANDING at the stove, Mother carefully dropped two eggs into boiling water. As the eggs poached, she measured half a cup of orange juice. She was wearing her lavender velour jogging suit and spotless Nikes. Her hair and makeup were perfect, if sprayed-stiff hair and a rainbow of eye shadow ranging from magenta to deep orange could be considered perfect. She opened and closed her mouth in a circular motion and bulged out her eyes—a morning ritual to prevent wrinkles.

"I'm making you breakfast . . . one hundred calories," she announced, "and then we'll go jogging. Just leave your diet to me for the next month and you'll be sleek as a model."

"I hate breakfast," I grouched. "It makes my face break out and I'm hungry for the rest of the day."

"Are you going to follow my advice?" she asked indignantly, "or do you want to remain a walrus?"

"Okay, okay," I muttered. "I'm too tired to argue." I figured that after a few days she'd forget about making breakfast because she's always late in the morning. The egg was soggy and tasteless. She grabbed the salt as soon as I reached for it.

"Dieting is like brushing your teeth. It's got to become a habit. No salt. Period." If there's one thing my mother is an expert on, it's dieting. I'm resolved to put myself in her hands. Once I lose weight, I'll never listen to another word she says.

At noon we drove to the athletic field. Mother demonstrated a series of stretching exercises. "This will limber you up," she said, bending down to grab her ankles and bouncing there. "One, two, three—reach up—touch the sky—down, two, three, four." Her hair remained fixed. Then I trundled after her as she bounded forward, her elbows bent at her sides, both hands flapping. She had a peculiar way of running—like the mincing gait of a circus pony.

A warm day, Indian summer lagging through November. The sun burnished the leaves pasted on the path. Golden leaves. I thought of the Mycenean necklace Mother and I had both coveted at the Metropolitan Museum in New York City.

"Remember the gold-leaf necklace?" I asked.

Mother nodded, concentrating on her breathing.

Four laps around constituted a mile. I laughed and horse-played next to her as she whacked me on the butt. Running the track: our truce time, these circles we run. Afterward the battle will rage on.

"You're going to look terrific," she said. "Just wait."

A couple in matching blue sweat suits sprinted ahead, followed by a waddling bulldog. The dog's tongue drooped out, his breathing was ragged. Rolls of fat shook as he wiggled his rear end and trotted off.

"What a disgusting-looking mutt," Mother said. She despises anything fat.

"He's so ugly, he's cute. I love his smashed-in face and roly-poly body."

"Vanessa . . . Vanessa Firestone." A tall, muscular man jogged over. His shaggy hair was held off his face by a sweatband. "I've been looking for you the last few days. I thought you might be getting lazy when you didn't show."

Mother slowed her pace and shot him a dazzling smile. "Hi, Barney. Meet my daughter, Jodie." We nodded at each other warily.

He mumbled, "How old are you?"

Mother said, "Fourteen," and I said, "Fifteen," at the same time.

"Actually, she's my baby-sitter," I remarked. Vanessa always wants people to think she's younger. Barney didn't even smile. His intentions toward Vanessa couldn't be honorable or he would at least pretend to laugh at my joke. Time to retreat. Vanessa was not smiling either.

Soon they were running together while I fell behind, gasping for breath. Four laps is my limit. Flopping on the grass next to the panting bulldog, I watched Mother and Barney lurch around the bend.

"We'll never make the Olympics, will we, old bully? But what about those two?" The dog snorted and rolled over. How I wished Barney hadn't shown up. Mother and I were having fun and along came Barney, the barnacle, and spoiled it. So that's why she spent an hour picking which jogging suit to wear. A new romance. Most of her romances fizzle after a few dates. I think her boyfriends take one look at my sullen face at the door and get discouraged. I never like any of them. They're either too old or too young. Mother doesn't seem overjoyed with her gentlemen callers either. But that's another subject we rarely discuss.

"I've become set in my ways," she said once. "It's hard enough sharing this apartment with you. I don't need to deal with another person's habits."

Barney invited us to have a cup of coffee. "Thanks anyway," I declined. He didn't look disappointed, but Mother did, as if she wished I would join them. Hesitating, she asked, "Where are you going, Jodie?"

"I'm going to Heather's." I don't like having to account for every move I make, but she's insistent.

"Well, write down exactly what you have for lunch," she commanded, linking her arm through Barney's. He ignored me, staring up at the sky and whistling.

"Don't worry. I'm not planning on having lunch," was my exit line. There's always so much going on at Heather's that I never think about eating . . . and then there's her brother, David. Just looking into his deep blue eyes makes me lose my appetite. The wonderful thing about David is that he doesn't know how wonderful he is. He always acts as if he values my opinion. Most boys make me uncomfortable. I'm sure they're thinking, "There's Jodie, the Firestone blimp." But not David. Talking with him is easy, except that half the time my heart is thudding, my face burning. For now I talk to David about art, his great love, and avoid mentioning my great love—him. I haven't told Heather how I feel. When I'm thin, I may confide in her.

Thoughts about David occupied me all the way across town to his house. When I turned into the Simmses' long, gravelly drive, he was sitting at his easel under their giant elm. He was so absorbed in his painting, he barely nodded. But I couldn't resist strolling over to him.

The russet leaves of the elm radiated a fiery brilliance. I watched David applying bronze daubs, transferring the fire to his canvas.

"What is it?" I asked, as if I didn't know.

"Amid these thick slashes of color, madam, is the essence of tree," David said in a professorial tone, even though he's only seventeen.

"The essence of tree? Sounds like a perfume."

"I'm trying to create an impression, not a photographic image." David added a quick stroke of purple, three vertical brown lines, and swirls of gold and orange.

I looked closer, and the lines emerged as three maidens dancing, bathed in a translucent glow, an autumn festival.

"Can I buy the painting when you're finished?" I asked shyly.

He grinned, surprised and pleased at the same time. "I'll give it to you, Jodie." And the way he said my name, stringing out the last syllable, made me glow inside as brightly as his canvas. I felt my face turning red. He continued to paint as I watched. He didn't seem to mind. When my mother's concentrating, she can't bear to have me nearby. My staring distracts her, she says. But I don't feel intrusive watching David work. He was wearing what he calls his genius clothes—white pants and a hand-woven poncho covered with paint stains. No one dresses the way he does. All the other boys at Hamilton wear a uniform: oxford button-down shirts, crew-neck sweaters, and corduroys. But David just wears what's comfortable: loose-fitting old clothes that can't be ruined by paint, chalk, or ink spots. He is unique and unassuming. I've watched him walk by the most beautiful girls in school without even acknowledging their stares. So far, David has been oblivious to his fan club. I hope he stays that way until I become tall and willowy. He even moves unselfconsciously. One day he accidentally tripped over a chair in the lunch room, and I could have sworn the chair said, "Excuse me."

Heather has the same kind of grace, a natural gift that allows her to be at ease in every social situation.

David applied a thin coat of burnt umber over the hot orange, giving the painting a veiled, mysterious look.

"Why did you do that?" I asked, shocked that he would obliterate the vibrant color.

"It's an experiment," he replied. "Bright colors are easy, too easy. Let the effect of color come through the shadows. If a risk isn't involved, then the problem's not worth solving."

Mr. Simms frowns on simple solutions, an attitude that has rubbed off on David—sometimes too much, if you ask me.

"So how's the budding Thespian?" he asked.

"I'm auditioning for the winter play—*Romeo and Juliet*. You ought to try out, too." Hint, hint! He'd be the perfect Romeo to my Juliet.

"Not a bad idea. I've always wanted to be in a play. If I don't make it, maybe I can help design the scenery." He underestimates himself. David makes the rest of the twerps that try out for school plays look like characters from Abbott and Costello movies.

When he turned back to his canvas, he started shaking

his head. "I messed up. Shouldn't have fooled with this picture any more. The burnt umber's all wrong." Disgusted with himself, David threw his brush on the grass. "I never know when to stop."

"But the painting's beautiful," I protested. "Don't say that."

A loud clash interrupted our conversation. It came from the second floor of the house. "Heather's twirling her baton," David said. "Probably smashed another light fixture."

"Your work is wonderful," I assured David and raced upstairs to find the latest victim of Heather's lethal baton.

"Look at this mess," moaned Heather, surrounded by shattered mirror glass in her bathroom. "I'm so keyed up I could hardly sleep last night."

Tomorrow the tryouts would be held for the regional twirling contest sponsored by the University of Connecticut. Heather and two hundred other girls from twenty-six neighboring high schools would be competing. The ten winners would lead the marching band at the homecoming game against State. The only subject that makes Heather jumpy, in more ways than one, is baton twirling. She'd been practicing her Little Joe flips, reverse figure eights, and fire trick for weeks. Smile, style, and sex appeal counted most, so Heather would win hands down.

She didn't believe me when I told her not to worry. I find her fascination with baton twirling totally incongruous with her more intellectual pursuits. Heather can't resist dressing in a sequined leotard and strutting to a Sousa march. She loves to hear her name announced at half time. It takes all my will power to stay and watch her instead of streaking out to be first in line at the hot-dog stand. Sometimes when I look down at the field and spot Heather, her face shining, her arms reaching to the sky, I feel a strange ache in my chest. There's more to it than simple envy. Seeing Heather at her bright moments makes me uncomfortably aware of all that I'm missing. I end up sneaking down and eating three hot dogs with mustard and relish.

Mr. Simms feels it his duty to encourage her, but I can tell he doesn't really approve. Heather knows it, too. Maybe twirling is her way of asserting her independence. Now Mr. Simms stomped into the room tooting on an imaginary horn.

"Good God, Heather, there's not a mirror, light bulb, or chandelier in the house that's safe. Jodie, I could hear the thump, thump of Heather practicing her routine at 2 a.m. She even tried to twirl that silly baton in the car yesterday. Her hands are swollen from handling it so much." Hugging Heather, he smoothed her hair. "Stop fretting. You'll make it."

Watching Mr. Simms comfort Heather made me want to cry. He was so tender with her.

"Enough is enough. Jodie, take Heather for a walk while I replace the light bulbs and clean this up." I laughed. Heather looked sheepish as we passed through the sliding glass doors, down railroad-tie stairs to the back yard. I looked to see if David was still around, but the elm blocked my view.

"I have to march in front of Sam Taylor, the baritone sax," Heather complained. "He keeps spitting on me."

"Why do you like twirling so much?" I asked Heather, who had the baton tucked under her arm like a rifle.

"I'm too short for basketball and baseball's boring. So what's left? Besides, I have fun even though you and Dad think it's dumb."

"Did I ever say that?"

"No, but I've seen you sneering during practice. You know I like working with those girls in the line."

She's right. I think "those girls" are a bunch of nincompoops—trying to catch the eye of every jock in the school. And their parents are worse, sitting at the sidelines of each game cheering, shouting instructions: "Stand up straight." "Keep in step." "Smile." One mother even bribed an official last year so her daughter could win in the competition. Competition—Heather enjoys that more than she'll admit.

"I've seen you out on that field," I teased, "grinning when your name is announced."

"Let's raid the icebox," suggested Heather, "and go on a picnic in the woods."

"I can't. I've just started a new diet." I wasn't hungry, but the word *icebox* produced images of Mrs. Simms's homemade cream pies.

"Maybe I should diet, too," said my emaciated friend. "Louise Lurie was eliminated from the preliminaries because she gained too much weight."

"I think a little baby fat in the right places would suit you," I said, poking her. Then I darted ahead and dove into a pile of leaves as she chased me, brandishing her baton. Hearing us squealing and shouting, David charged over to join us. Soon we were hurling leaves at each other and scrambling in the piles, neatly raked by poor Mr. Simms that morning. When David toppled me over on the grass and tousled my hair with the soft leaves, I was filled with

31

such wild, silly happiness that I wanted to pull him down with me. Instead I stuffed leaves down his shirt.

"So you're going to play rough." He laughed, and landed right on top of me, rolling us down the hill.

As soon as I felt his body against mine, I stiffened with embarrassment. I didn't want him to know how big and fat I was. Like a feather bed—that's what I must feel like! A big, mushy mattress! I shoved him away.

Quickly jumping up, he brushed himself off and stalked back to the house. I didn't know if he was mad or just grossed out. For the rest of the day I was afraid to look him in the eyes.

5

A whopper at Burger King is 630 calories. A fifteen-piece bucket of Colonel Sanders' Kentucky Fried is 3,300 calories, and a hot fudge brownie delight sundae is a rousing 580 at the corner Dairy Queen. High Ridge is franchise Shangri-la. Consequently the only restaurant in town that Vanessa has not decreed off limits is Mr. Wheatley's Health Food Store on the corner of Sixth and Pine. Surrounded by drab storefronts, the shop has a bright green façade. Inside is a clean, cozy café run meticulously by Mr. Wheatley. Booths upholstered in shiny yellow vinyl with white knobby wooden tables line the walls. Basking in an aroma of cinnamon tea and baked apples, I usually sit on a stool at the counter to chat with Mr. Wheatley. There I indulge myself in a bean-sprout sandwich on diet whole wheat for 150 calories, with hot tea for dessert. Mr. Wheatley is big on roughage. I think he's in cahoots with my mother. Bran flakes, that's the magic ingredient.

"The success of crash diets should be taken with a grain of salt," advised Mr. Wheatley. "No pun intended." He generously sprinkled bran on my sprouts. Bending over my plate, I pretended to faint from hunger. A rosy-cheeked dwarf with a halo of silver hair, he's only five feet tall and resembles *Snow White*'s Doc. In the last three weeks Mr. Wheatley and I had become great friends. Whereas my mother checks every biteful, barks instructions on nutrition, and accuses me of cheating, Mr. Wheatley is always encouraging. I've already lost nine pounds. Only eleven more and my ideal weight will be achieved, one hundred pounds. Staggering into the Health Food Store after school, I consume my daily sandwich slowly, chewing each morsel as if it's my last, while Mr. Wheatley philosophizes.

"This culture has become food-suggestible," he told me, vigorously wiping off the tables. "Animals get hungry, they eat. When they're full, they stop. We eat whether we're hungry or not." He paused to reflect on this profundity.

"You're absolutely right," I agreed. "I used to eat desserts even after stuffing myself at dinner. I watched television and automatically went to the refrigerator during commercials. I couldn't pass a bakery without going in and gobbling a sweet roll or cupcake." I still have to pass Schneider's Pastry Shop quickly. I'm surrounded by temptation—Heather inviting me over to make chocolate chip cookies; pizza binges after Friday night football games; popcorn at the movies. It's giving me a bad case of the pig-out blues. My friends eat all they want and stay slim. I can't even look at food without gaining weight. But I've remained strong, stalwart, a model of self-restraint with the looming figure of Vanessa Firestone standing guard.

My only problem, aside from hunger, is that I'm so exhausted that I drag myself out of bed every morning and nearly sleep through classes. My diet consists of Vanessa's breakfast, which she insists on fixing every morning, much to my surprise. Then juice for lunch, a sprout sandwich after school, and two carrots, a cucumber (no salt), two hard-boiled eggs, plus a tiny slice of chicken for dinner. For dessert, I get a half of a grapefruit (no sugar). I swallow a laxative, stagger into bed at 7:30 p.m., listen to my stomach rumble, and fall asleep until the alarm rings at 7:30 a.m. This has been going on for twenty days. The audition is in one week.

No one has noticed a difference yet except me, Mr. Wheatley, and Vanessa, who's keeping track of the pounds on a chart. I guess people have a fixed image of a fat Jodie Firestone. Besides, I am still hiding under my thick sweater and baggy jeans. But on stage, as the houselights dim, there will be a sudden shock of recognition as a slender Juliet, vaguely resembling me, emerges from the shadows.

"How does this sound?" I asked Mr. Wheatley. " 'Good night, good night! Parting is such . . . *sweet* . . . sorrow.' "

"Try it this way," he said. "Good night, good night . . . *Sweetie*, parting is such sorrow."

"But Shakespeare put the adjective before the sorrow. You've changed the whole meaning of the line."

"Well, how about this," he suggested, his blue eyes twinkling. "Good night, good night! How sweet it is . . . such sorrow!"

"Shakespeare is probably turning over in his grave," I told him, grabbing my knapsack and waving goodbye.

"Good night, good night," trailed after me in his mock-tragic voice.

Another cold, rainy day. High Ridge is plagued with the foggiest weather in Connecticut. Between the chemical plant, the munitions factory, and the airport two miles out of town, we rarely see a blue sky. A smoky sky indicates a clear day.

Myrna was just leaving our apartment when I arrived. I could smell her musk-oil perfume.

"Jodie, I hid a frozen custard pie for you in your bedroom. Your mother is going to starve you to death." She was wearing a dyed green rabbit fur and purple cowboy boots. Her sticky, lip-glossed kiss bounced off my cheek like a rubber plunger.

"Don't worry about it, Myrna. I want to lose weight."

"You look fine," she said. "Your mother makes too much of your weight. I like chubby little girls."

"You're the only one who does," I retorted. Somehow the way she said that bothered me. I politely told her I'd look for the pie, but I made a mental note to pitch it as soon as she left.

But, with the stance of a Bengal lancer, Vanessa blocked my door—holding the pie. She glared at me accusingly. I didn't want to rat on Myrna, but neither did I want to be blamed for the frozen Sara Lee special. What if I took the pie and splattered it in her face? An image of a burlesque routine flashed through my head. "Makeup," calls the comedian. Then he gets the pie right in the kisser.

"At the next football game, while your friend Heather struts around wiggling her fanny, you'll be in the stands stuffing your fat face and taking up two seats," she growled. Oh yes, right in the kisser.

When Vanessa mentions Heather, I know she's trying to start trouble, make me hate my best friend. It's a strain not to be influenced. After all, I'd have to be completely dense not to notice Heather has more going for her than I

36

do. Yet we've never tried to compete. I've seen enough of that at school between girls who spend so much time fighting over boys that they turn bitchy and boring, always talking behind each other's backs. I don't want that kind of friendship with Heather. Yet Mother always manages to raise doubts. Maybe Heather likes me because I'm no threat. The only way to stop myself from being suspicious is to remember all the times Heather's helped me and the way we make each other laugh.

Still at the door glowering, Vanessa waited for me to rise to her bait.

"Out of my room," I commanded. "And take that crummy pie with you. The only way it could have gotten in here was by a *deus ex machina*." I never gave her the satisfaction of a straight answer.

Vanessa strode off, lips curled in anger. I was too weak even to cry. She's jealous of Heather and the whole Simms family, because they have everything we don't . . . and the list is long. When Heather made the twirling finals, Vanessa could have wrapped the baton around Heather's neck. She railed about that for two days.

"You better win something," she screamed. "That will show them." *Them*—an ambiguous term for all the people in High Ridge who shopped at Trumbells and treated my mother like a lowly salesclerk.

I'd like to show "them" too—and someday I will. But not now. I collapsed on my bed while visions of custard pie danced through my head.

6

Some misguided buyer from Trumbells had made a deal with a Japanese exporter. Sliding through bamboo doors, I found myself in a facsimile of a Japanese pagoda. The main floor had been transformed into an oriental bazaar. Paradise, if one had a penchant for embroidered scarves, silk robes, scrolls, screens, lacquered furniture, and other miscellany from paper parasols to dragon kites. Paradise Lost, if one craved the all-around American-girl look.

"I'm not leaving here decked out like a geisha girl," I hissed to Vanessa, who plucked a mandarin-collared dress with side slits from a rack and held it up to me.

The sales personnel, garbed in obis and bedroom slippers, stood in silly splendor. Floating above us was a huge banner that read: MADE IN JAPAN—as if we didn't know. Salamander-colored walls, music from *Madame Butterfly*, and Mr. Kramer, the store manager, modeling crimson silk pajamas, completed the tableau. Open-mouthed, I strolled past china knickknacks, hundreds of hibachis, rice-paper lanterns, plastic fans, and a karate demonstration.

"A grand Grand Opening to announce Trumbells's new image," raved Mr. Kramer. "We're offering group Zen lessons, origami for the tots, flower arranging, and free shrimp tempura recipes."

"I prefer chop suey," I remarked. Vanessa tried to repress a snicker. Kramer complains when he has to pay for overtime or rearrange her work schedule. Even though he takes advantage of her, she's afraid to offend him. Kramer was preening like a cockatoo in a gleeful twitter over what appeared to be the most eye-boggling display since McDonald's opened in High Ridge with a Ronald McDonald look-alike contest.

"Have a tantalizing tidbit," Kramer crooned, offering us an egg roll. I was famished, my mouth watered, but I didn't dare take it in front of Vanessa.

"Go ahead, Jodie." Mother grabbed several tasties from the tray. "You deserve a treat. Jodie's lost almost twenty pounds," she proudly proclaimed. "We're here to revamp her entire wardrobe."

"Don't overlook these imported treasures," advised Kramer. "How about an ornamental comb, a Suga jump suit, or a guaranteed, genuine Sung Dynasty robe?"

"Maybe I'm just dense, Mr. Kramer," I said sweetly, "but aren't you mixing your cultures? Sung Dynasty and egg rolls are Chinese."

"Aren't you the smart one?" Kramer pouted, pursing his lips and sputtering off. His hands fluttered nervously; his pajama bottoms drooped. Mother and I burst out laughing.

As Vanessa stalked the aisles hunting for suitable garments for her starving but almost skinny daughter, I noticed the lecherous glances she got from the salesmen. Winking at one, pinching the cheek of another, Mother clearly enjoyed being the belle of Trumbells.

"Aren't there any normal clothes here?" I complained.

"Mrs. Firestone," called a woman, sweeping grandly toward us. A swirl of white fur and feathers, she was loaded with packages. "I need to return these items immediately."

"I'm not on duty today," replied Vanessa curtly. Shedding a trail of white feathers, the lady puffed away indignantly.

"A raving lunatic," muttered Vanessa. "I spend hours waiting on her as she pulls out every item in the department; she charges a thousand dollars' worth and returns it all the next day."

"Do you deal with many customers like that?" I asked, realizing how difficult her job must be. If only Kramer appreciated how valuable my mother is. She has more savvy than anyone in the whole store.

"My regular clients are fine," she answered, "but the loonies are irresistibly attracted to me and Kramer's motto is 'The customer's always right.' What really bothers me is that I'm supposed to be a buyer but I end up waiting on people half the time."

"I'd register a complaint with the president of the company," I suggested. "You and Myrna should start an affirmative-action program."

"Myrna and I are hardly indispensable. We'd both be out of a job."

"Then find a better one," I tossed out. For all Vanessa's assertiveness with me, she was timid about defending her own rights.

"It's not that easy," Vanessa mumbled, and I realized how boxed in she must feel. A thankless job—not only here but at home. I resolved to be co-operative today. But at the

Teen Center I grew gloomy. Too many plaids and checks —materials that reminded me of the dull chatter of Heather's cheerleader friends. Too much the conventional costume of Hamilton High. With those clothes I'd blend in with the other brown wrens. I wanted my new plumage to be gay, unusual clothes that would inspire a siren's song or the mating call of a whooping crane. The racks bulged with outfits that symbolized sock hops, colonial houses, boarding schools, and Boston. To please Vanessa, I settled on one plaid jumper, a blazer, and a pair of blue slacks, size 8! Then I picked a wild print dress with pleats, ruffles, and puffy sleeves, a diaphanous long scarf, and a fluffy green angora dress on sale.

Hovering in the dressing room, Vanessa could hardly conceal her delight as I observed my new reflection in the mirror.

"I'm not Jackie O.," I told her, "but my next purchase may be a bikini."

"Remember to suck in your stomach and learn to smile without that toothy grin." Vanessa was at it again. Why did she have to spoil every decent moment we had together?

"So now I don't smile the right way?" I demanded.

"I've just spent a queen's ransom on you. I'm allowed a few constructive suggestions." Who did you buy these things for, I asked silently, me or you?

"Your advice is so constructive, I may never smile again." Sullenly I motioned her out. Scrutinizing my face in the mirror, I practiced my smile. First, a sultry Brooke Shields pout, followed by a lascivious leer. With my lips puckered, I was a peevish vixen.

I gave up, back to my "toothy grin." Stop this charade, I scolded myself. Why are you letting Vanessa rankle you again? Now that I'm a normal weight, she's discovering new material to pick apart: my pug nose, bushy eyebrows, ragged fingernails, big feet. She'll dissect all my bodily parts, performing verbal surgery. "Whose body is this anyway?" I wanted to shout through the curtain, down the long dressing-room aisle. "I'm in charge of your body," Vanessa would answer, "and don't you forget it!"

7

Mr. Wuensche is the intense, bespectacled teacher who directs the Drama Guild. His plays, called Wuensche's Wonders, are always plagued by crises: the principal will not put up the money for costumes, the stage lighting is faulty. His choice of plays is criticized—*Romeo and Juliet*, for example, is considered improper.

"*Taming of the Shrew* might be bawdy," commented Mrs. Drabble, "but at least it's funny." She's right. There are few laughs in *Romeo and Juliet*.

Miss Whiting, our English teacher, hates the play. "A young girl giving herself away on a hunch, like an animal. It's indecent."

But the real plagues of Wuensche's existence are auditions. Practically half the school wants to be in the play because rehearsals are a legitimate excuse to cut class. Yet very few students ever show up for Drama Guild meetings.

On audition day, fifty people crowded into the Little Theater. Wuensche had to give everyone a turn to read. If he chose only Drama Guild members, he'd be accused of favoritism.

The Little Theater was built three years ago, along with

a new gym, as a result of an addendum to a school tax amendment. The taxpayers thought they were voting to boost the athletic department of Hamilton High. The theater was an afterthought. The stage is built on a hexagonal slant with seats on five sides—theater in the round, ideal for a Shakespearean production.

I scanned the room for Mr. Wuensche. He was in the front row with a harassed expression on his long face and a notebook clenched in his hands. Bensinger sprawled next to him. For the last year I had been Wuensche's script girl, organizer, and occasional actress at practice sessions. He counted on me to make sure everyone was present for rehearsals, that costumes and makeup were in order and publicity circulated. Only juniors and seniors get the leads, so now it was my turn. When I slipped into the empty seat beside him, his eyes widened, puzzled at first, then he smiled.

"Jodie, let me guess which part you're trying for."

I smiled back. My long, brown hair was looped into braids with a garland of flowers around my head. My costume was a long, white Empire robe borrowed from Vanessa. I hadn't reached my magic weight yet, but almost. My face was so pale that I had to apply blush to my cheeks. I'd not eaten for twenty-four hours. Bensinger's long jaw dropped with surprise when he realized who I was.

"Lookin' good, Jodie," he said.

I nodded and pretended to be absorbed in the script, which I knew by heart.

Wuensche let five people do a scene together, beginning with volunteers. Drama Guild members must go last, so there would be a long, tedious wait.

The room was hot and stuffy. My throat felt parched, my stomach queasy from nerves and hunger. The readings droned endlessly. Shakespeare's poetry was scrambled and fried, chopped and mangled. Mr. Wuensche moaned every now and then.

I spotted David Simms sauntering in and caught his eye. He grinned and bounded over.

"Jodie, you look terrific. Heather told me you've been eating bean sprouts for weeks." He smelled like shellac, but to me it was an aphrodisiac.

"David, meet Mr. Wuensche."

"Glad to meet you, sir," said David Simms in his casual, friendly voice. Relaxed, sincere, he was a contrast to Bensinger, who had been bowing and scraping to Wuensche all year.

"Ah yes, the artist," remarked Wuensche. "I've seen your work displayed in the halls. Maybe you'd like to help design sets."

"Sure," replied David, "but I'd like to read for a part first if that's all right with you."

"Read away, young man. You can go on next."

Bensinger shifted in his seat, a look of disdain on his face. He had condescended to audition for Romeo and he sensed competition. "My last gift to Hamilton High," he told me last week. I tried to imagine kissing him in the balcony scene, and gagged.

David hopped agilely on stage, followed by a girl I didn't know, a story-book creature with an elfin, heart-shaped face, luminous brown eyes, and thick, black hair streaming down her back. David offered his hand to help her up. She didn't say thank you, just nodded coolly and faced the audience. I wondered if it was coincidental that this small-boned beauty and David were auditioning together.

"I'm Maude St. James," she announced in clipped tones.

"I've just moved to High Ridge or I would have joined Drama Guild months ago." Maude St. James—a romantic name—complete with a British accent and the sultry air of Tess of the D'Urbervilles. My response was immediate. "I have a faint cold fear thrills through my veins, / That almost freezes up the heat of life," I whispered from Juliet's famous soliloquy. Grasping the arms of the chair, I gritted my teeth. She faltered several times during the reading, but David was so smooth, as if he always talked in iambic pentameter, that he made her look wonderful. The energy created between them was impressive, and Mr. Wuensche scribbled notes for the first time in two hours. Maybe they just seemed good because all the morons before them were so terrible.

Bensinger swore and frantically studied his lines. I wished Mr. Wuensche would give us a break before our audition. Some time was necessary to compose myself, to fight the waves of nausea that had been washing over me for hours.

David and Maude St. James exited stage right, together. He gestured energetically. Miss Coffee, Tea, or Crumpets was still nodding coolly.

The rest, as the magazines say, is history. Bensinger and I were the only two left to audition. On stage, I felt a dizzying pain between my eyes. Before I even had a chance to swallow the poison and say, "Romeo, I come! This do I drink to thee," I blacked out, passed out cold on Juliet's bed. Curtain.

I woke up in the nurse's office with the garland of flowers on a table next to my face. The white dress with me inside was crumpled on a cot while Heather, David, and Mr. Wuensche looked on anxiously.

"Is this Juliet's funeral pyre?" I managed to quip. "Where's my dagger?"

"Are you all right?"

"You fainted! We were going to call an ambulance."

"Girl, you're absolutely weak from hunger. You could get seriously ill starving yourself that way."

"What you need is a hot meal and a week in bed."

"You were terrific," I said to David. He didn't look very pleased. Mr. Wuensche looked pained.

"Let me talk to Jodie a few minutes alone," he told them, and then Wuensche was sitting on the edge of the cot facing me, holding my hand, which lay sweaty and limp in his.

"We start rehearsals tomorrow and you're in no shape to act, much less do anything else. I'm saving the part of the Nurse for you, anyway," he said, "and you and Bensinger will be my co-directors."

Script girl again. A skeleton of my former self to play the part of the fat old Nurse. I wanted to scream. Instead I pulled my hand away and I stared at him wordlessly.

Finally I asked, "Who will be Juliet?"

"Probably the new girl from London. Maude St. James. She and David worked well together. Listen, Jodie, I know how disappointed you must be, but you aren't up to anything strenuous, not until you gain your strength back."

Still I didn't respond. What good would it do now? All my starving, exercising, listening to Vanessa's boring spiels on nutrition had obviously been useless. I sank back on the pillow, fighting tears, and mustered up a resigned, good-sportsmanlike smile. It was my greatest performance.

"I guess I won't be needing this." I shoved the crown on the floor. Wuensche tried to take my hand again, but it was clear that he couldn't wait to make his escape. "I think I'd better call my mother," I said, giving him an excuse to leave.

He backed out of the room. "Come to rehearsals as soon as you're feeling up to it. We'll hold off on your scenes." His enthusiasm sounded phony, but I managed a sweet thank-you, even though at that moment my head was a hornet's nest, buzzing with fury at Wuensche. When David came back into the room with Heather, I hated him, too. David's not insensitive. He must have guessed my mood because he awkwardly handed me a package wrapped in newspaper and quickly took off.

"David rushed home to get this," Heather said.

I opened it, sensing that the canvas he had been working on beneath the elm would be inside, my consolation prize while he and Maude St. James became the greatest lovers of all time. Alone with Heather, I sobbed. There were no clever remarks left. How could I have believed being thin would change anything? After putting my hand on my flat, empty stomach, I wiped my nose with my sleeve and sat up. I felt hungry now, with a hunger that could be filled in only one way. I felt like eating myself into oblivion. Heather was speaking in even, soothing tones.

"You could be the greatest Juliet in the world. That sour puss Maude will be awful."

"When did she turn up?" I asked. "I've never seen her around before."

"Her father's a professor of economics at the University of London and he's here on sabbatical."

"Why here in High Ridge of all places?"

"Because Maude's family owns the land next to our barn and they've moved into the farmhouse there. They're fixing it up."

I glared at Heather as if this British invasion were her doing. "Next to your house?" I couldn't believe it. "How did she find out about the audition so quickly?"

Heather looked down and then I knew that Maude and David had met before, that he was the one who'd brought her to the Little Theater. I was glad I'd never told Heather about my crush on David, that would only have added to my disgrace.

"Let's get out of here. I've never felt like a bigger mess. That dumb diet! Vanessa and her damn raw vegetables! What a wasted effort!"

"That's not true," said Heather. "You look so good now."

I didn't look good. She was lying to make me feel better.

"You can even eat pizza without worrying."

"Maybe that's just what I'll do."

"Come home with me instead. Mother will give you the best dinner you've eaten in weeks."

But I couldn't face David again. I wanted to be alone.

"Thanks anyway, but I think I'd better head home."

On the way back to our apartment, I stopped at Burger Chef. I dreaded having to tell Vanessa what had happened. She'd never let me hear the end of it. The familiar smell of french fries and hamburger on the griddle was just what I'd been craving; yet the odor made me nauseous all over again. My mouth wanted food but my stomach didn't. Still, I ordered two double cheeseburgers to go. I snuck up to my rooftop hideaway and nursed my sorrows with processed cheese and a gooey hamburger on a sesame-seed bun.

8

THERE was a scene with Vanessa over my grades. And she was furious that I didn't get the part, as if I had fainted on purpose. The fight began with her screaming and ended with her screaming. In the middle I screamed, too; but I didn't cry. All the while sirens were blaring down Main Street, perfect background music for us to play out our drama. When we finished shrieking, we both retreated to our rooms and haven't said a word to each other since. That was a week ago. I won't go back to school; in fact, when Mother leaves for work in the morning, I stay in bed. When she returns in the evening, I'm still there. In between, I sneak out to stock up on food, charged to various grocery stores around town. She hasn't received the bills yet. When they come, she'll raise a cry that will cause an earth tremor on Main Street.

Meanwhile, I cover my tracks by cooking frozen pizzas and TV dinners with the windows open to dispel the odor, and by emptying the trash before she returns. I don't think about anything except food, how to procure, eat, and hide it. Under my bed I keep bags of potato chips and cookies. Vanessa doesn't dare to search my room now. I store the frozen items on the roof. In layers of clothing, a sweat suit, a flannel robe, and a grubby old plaid poncho, I pad around the apartment. Like a squirrel gathering nuts for the winter, or a big rubber bear, I had room to stretch, to grow. I was in hiding.

Vanessa's charts, books, and lists were dumped back in her corner of the house. I didn't step on the scale any more. David's painting was propped up against the wall as a grim reminder of my theatrical fiasco. Eventually I'd have to go back to school, but my blackout at the Little Theater gave me the excuse to call in sick, to forge a note from Vanessa informing the principal that "Jodie is recuperating at home, gaining her strength back."

Someone came by once, but I ignored the doorbell. It may sound as if I was having some kind of nervous breakdown, but I knew exactly what I was doing. My mind and body were my own to do whatever I wanted with, and what I wanted was to be left alone, to be mindless, and, most important, not to be hungry any more. Every food fantasy that occurred during my starvation diet I indulged myself in. I was in Milky Way heaven, I was a bottomless pit. It didn't start out that way. Even though I was hiding out, I resolved not to become fat again. Just one piece of candy, I would tell myself, and pretty soon I'd gobbled down the whole bag. After a while I gave up and was back to my old habits.

During the long afternoons I napped with the stereo blaring. In the evening there was sweet silence. Vanessa would come home, shower, fuss over her hair and clothes, and then go out—presumably with Barney, whose low Southern drawl was instantly recognizable. When Vanessa returned, I was sound asleep.

One night I had a revelation. I'd stick it out until I was

sixteen, and then take off. But being on my own would require money, which I definitely didn't have. All day I tried to think of where to find a job. It was my only motivation for getting out of the house besides my scavenger hunts for food. People could call me a sore loser, a spoilsport, just feeling sorry for myself. Fine. Let them say what they wanted. But I had plans. New York! Come spring, that was where I'd be headed. Only two hours by train. Goodbye, High Ridge. Goodbye, Vanessa. The next time Wuensche saw my name, it would be lit up on a billboard over Broadway.

Noon. The bells from the Presbyterian Church were my signal. Time to make lunch, even though my last snack was less than an hour before. Okay, just one can of Hormel chili. But then I found myself opening another can, and suddenly a quart of chocolate mint ice cream disappeared. I felt sick, but ready or not, I had to make my foray into the industrial district of High Ridge. Somewhere within the walls of the various smoke-stacked plants was a job for an ambitious young adult willing to accept below the minimum wage for services rendered. A young adult with a premature pot belly.

Changing my attire for the first time in days, I was surprised that my new slacks still fit, although I had to suck my stomach in to zip them up. But with one step forward, the zipper ripped. Back to my old khakis, which were a little loose but comfortable. A turtleneck sweater and blazer made me look officially presentable. After stuffing my dirty hair into Vanessa's felt beret, I ventured forth onto the familiar drab streets of High Ridge. The sidewalks were crowded with shopgirls, clerks, and office workers on their lunch break.

How could I dare to walk into some unknown person's business and wangle a job? How could I even begin? Should I get down on my hands and knees and beg? Never! Should I march in and impress them by my bold manner and dashing style? Determined, I quickened my pace, but despite my cocky demeanor, my confidence was slipping away. In its place was a dull fear. Of what? I didn't know. Maybe of failing again. I had never been good at first impressions. I'm the kind of person that grows on someone, like an odd, abstract painting. After a while the shapes and colors make sense, but at first glance one sees a disconnected, unidentifiable mass.

I looked at the people who brushed by me, heading for their routine places. They seemed to be snickering, "Where are you going, little girl?" Nowhere. I trudged along, my footsteps moving slower and slower. As I turned a corner, I bumped into Myrna Hochman, emerging from HoJo's.

"Glad to see you up," she began. "Your mother tells me you haven't been out of bed for a week." She gave me the once-over. "Your face is looking better, fuller. The old roundness is reappearing." Her voice had the cloying quality of a praline.

"You were much too gaunt. Not at all compatible with your personality." I wondered why she needed to sabotage her best friend's mania for having a thin daughter. Sometimes I thought she was jealous of Vanessa.

"You and I were never meant to be skeletal like your mother."

Righto, you maddening mannequin. I need all the encouragement I can get.

She sashayed past me, hips swinging, smiling at a gray-flanneled executive type, who avoided looking back. Even during her lunch hour she's on the prowl.

Seeing Myrna, so full of sugar-coated ill will, reminded me of my mother. My determination to find a way out came surging back. Half-running, I passed the office buildings and department stores that lined the short stretch of highway that led to the textile factory. SKULLY BROTHERS MANUFACTURERS the faded black and white sign read. The plant was a series of low concrete and glass buildings in the shape of a horseshoe. The glass was silver so you could not see in, but they could see out. A two-story structure in the middle looked like the main office. An uglier group of buildings I'd never seen. Not a plant, bush, or tree on the outside. Instead of grass, gravel lined the cement walks and paved parking lots.

Pushing through the wooden door, I found myself facing a wire gate with a buzzer. Inside were several empty desks and a tall, slope-shouldered man standing at a filing cabinet. He reminded me of a long caterpillar. I rang the bell and the doors slid open. The man and I looked at each other in silence for a long moment. Finally he removed a cigar from his mouth and addressed me in a snappy, severe voice with a definite Brooklyn accent.

"What do you want?" he asked. Not a welcoming tone, but I refused to be discouraged.

"I'm looking for part-time work," I replied, looking directly into his squinty blue eyes.

"We don't need part-timers," he said sternly. "Too many

people can work eight hours a day. How old are you anyway, young lady?"

"Eighteen," I lied.

"What exactly can you do?" Some question! I hardly knew. I mean, I hardly knew then who I was. I might have known the last week or even last year, but right then I was in a state of flux.

"I'm not sure. I'm willing to try anything."

"What do you mean? Can you file, type, take shorthand?" His questions came flying like guided missiles and I was the target. I shook my head.

"All you young people," he continued in a mournful tone, "always looking for jobs, but you can't do anything. Not even spell or write a complete sentence. You'd better learn to do something or at least have an idea how to be useful before you come around asking for work, wasting my time."

I couldn't think of a thing to say back to him except how are teenagers supposed to learn unless we're given a chance to try? He was an old ogre, looking at me contemptuously, so I turned to leave.

"Come back here, young lady," he called. That sounded more promising, so I faced him again. He stood there puffing away on his foul-smelling cigar, peering at me with folded hands. Finally he pulled the cigar out of his mouth and said, "My boy pushed drugs, rioted for peace, and disappeared eight years ago. Haven't heard from him since. Crazy kid, he was a real disappointment to his mother and me. I don't want any teenagers working around the office. No offense, miss, but you make me think of my boy." He ground his cigar out in the plastic ashtray on his desk, sank into his chair, and swiveled around until his back faced me.

That's probably what Vanessa Firestone will say someday, too. "Crazy kid disappeared. A real disappointment."

With a father like you, I wanted to shout at the balding head bent over the desk, I don't blame your son for running away. Clanking the wire gate shut, I felt my hands trembling. The man flicked his fingers in another gesture of dismissal.

"I would never work for you anyway," I blurted out. I ran into the dusty parking lot, pulled the beret down over my ears, and rushed back toward town. I wasn't even disappointed. High Ridge is hardly full of possibilities, I mean, for finding employment or fighting ennui, and every encounter I had convinced me that it was the most impossible place in the world to live. I should get out of here as soon as possible. Explore every possibility. My head was teeming with possibilities, none of them clear or even describable. But I knew as I crossed the intersections, past yellow lights, past playgrounds, shops, back yards, and bus stops, finally perching myself on the counter at Mr. Wheatley's Health Food Store, that there was nothing and nobody to hold me here.

"I'll have a triple rice burger with Swiss cheese," I told Mr. Wheatley. "No more seaweed for me! And definitely hold the bran flakes."

Mr. Wheatley said, "Yes, ma'am!" and saluted me, but he looked puzzled. When I slipped off my parka, his mouth turned down in a way that reflected a kind of sadness. He seemed to sense my state, but I knew he wouldn't ask any prying questions. Soon I began to spill the whole story, from my four weeks on hunger strike, to the botched audition, to my thwarted job interview at the factory.

He listened quietly, his head cocked to one side, stirring his tea with slow strokes. Finally he said thoughtfully, "Mrs. Wheatley and I opened this place together. She was a great believer in what she called pure food. We had a lovely vegetable garden, grew our own herbs, and never ate meat, even before the vegetarian craze. She urged me to open this place when I retired from the Army, and we ran it together until she died last year. I couldn't bring myself to close, nor could I hire anyone else to help me. Mrs. Wheatley had her own way of running things, special blends for tea, just the right amount of time for soup to simmer before adding a secret ingredient. Somehow I couldn't see anyone else coming in here and changing things." He paused and poured me another cup of jasmine tea.

"I wish I had known Mrs. Wheatley," I said. "She sounds so wonderful."

"Jodie, some afternoons when it's quiet in here and the sun filters through the windows and streaks shadows on the walls, and I'm listening to the classical music she loved, I can almost see her bustling around, straightening up, scolding me because the counter's not sparkling clean . . ." His voice trailed off and he pulled out a handkerchief and blew his nose. "Well, what I'm trying to say," he said when he had recovered, "is that I could use some help here in the afternoons and on Saturdays. This place isn't crowded during the day, but around dinnertime every health nut in town stops by for a snack. You might be the right person to give me a hand."

I looked at him in amazement. Me? He wanted *me* to work for him?

Mrs. Wheatley wouldn't approve at all, I thought. I'm too messy, and if Mr. Wheatley ever knew about my junk food sprees . . . But still, I was actually being offered a real job.

"I couldn't pay you much," came Mr. Wheatley's voice. "But would three dollars an hour suit you?"

"Suit me!" I cried. "That's way too much."

He laughed. "I can tell you'd make a great business-woman. Three dollars is a fair wage, Jodie, and that's what I'm willing to pay. Two hours, three afternoons a week, and six hours on Saturdays."

"It's a deal," I said, thrusting my hand across the counter and shaking his warm, chubby paw. He squeezed back hard. And I promised myself right then and there that I wouldn't disappoint him. Yet in the back of my mind there was a strange, gnawing doubt, as if something could happen to spoil our plan. I ordered a piece of apple cinnamon pie, wolfed it down, letting my mind dwell on the spicy, apple flavor instead of fear that I would disappoint Mr. Wheatley. I arrived home just in time to shut the door of my room before I heard my mother's key in the lock.

9

"A RESTAURANT!" screamed Vanessa. "You have a job in a restaurant? Ridiculous! Just what you need, to be surrounded by food all the time. I won't allow it."

"You've been harping on me for months to find a job. Now I have one and you won't allow it. I don't believe this. Mr. Wheatley's is the only place you let me eat on my diet." I was furious, but I tried to keep my voice calm. I didn't want to let this conversation take on our usual pattern: screaming, tears, then silence. Nothing accomplished. I had to stay calm.

"Food is all you think or talk about," continued Vanessa. "The Health Food Store couldn't be a worse place for you, especially since you've lost weight and I've spent a month's salary outfitting you." She stomped back and forth across the kitchen. "Besides, I didn't raise my daughter to be a waitress."

So that was it! A job at Mr. Wheatley's Health Food Store symbolized everything she hated. Food equaled fat; a job as a waitress equaled social inferiority. I tried to view her objectively, as if she were a stranger with whom I had no connection, as if she were one of her nasty customers at Trumbells. Reason with her. Don't get ruffled, I told myself.

"Helping Mr. Wheatley out, as an assistant, the way he and Mrs. Wheatley used to work together, is what I'll be doing. Besides, you know the food he serves isn't fattening."

"Anything is fattening," she retorted, "if you eat too much of it."

"Mr. Wheatley's a wonderful man. I like him. He's done a lot for me."

"Oh, so you like him," she said, her voice becoming shrill again. "And you don't like me, I do nothing for you? Mr. Wheatley this, Mr. Wheatley that. I'm sick of hearing his name."

"You don't want me to have friends," I began to shout. "You've never wanted me to have friends. You don't have a nice word for anyone. I can't bring my friends home because you're so nasty to them. I don't know what you want of me." None of it made sense any more. What was wrong with me that nothing I did pleased her? When I was little, she wouldn't let me out of her sight; yet now she couldn't stand the sight of me. Still she wouldn't let go, wouldn't leave me alone.

I reached for the box of bran flakes. She slapped my hand, and suddenly something snapped. I began hurling cereal all over the room. Pushing and shoving her, I started shrieking and crying.

"I hate you! I hate you! You want to kill me! You wish I were dead!"

Vanessa tried to grab my wrists, but I was stronger than she was. I could feel myself forcing her into the living room. Arms flailing, gasping, wild-eyed, I struck at the softness of her breasts, the rigidity of her arms. I almost knocked her down on the couch. It was when I realized that I could overpower her that I finally stopped screaming and pushing.

60

"You're crazy," she hissed at me, crumpling on the couch. "I have a crazy daughter." Then she staggered into her bedroom and closed the door. Next I heard her dialing the phone, talking in low, unintelligible tones. I shook all over. I could still feel the impact of my mother's hard frame, and the sickening feeling of being out of control.

I wondered if she was calling the hospital to come lock me up. How did this happen? I am not well. I don't know how this happened, but I am not well. I should be sorry, full of remorse, but instead a sense of jubilation overwhelmed me. Later I may feel guilty, disgusted that I'm capable of behaving so horribly; but right now I know if Vanessa were to come out of that room and yell at me, I would have to shove her all over again.

Some strange impulse made me take five dollars out of her purse. Crumpling the bill in my fist, I slammed out of the apartment. The fat little kid from the flat down the hall was coming up the stairs. He stuck out his tongue. Grabbing him by the collar, I snarled, "Do that again, you little jerk, and I'll flatten you." He pulled away and ran past me. I am a menace, the bully of High Ridge.

Five dollars at Burger King goes a long way. A feast of grease. I lost myself, spaced out on french fries, catsup, and cheeseburgers. When I returned to the apartment, there was only the familiar dusty smell of worn furniture to greet me. Vanessa's door was closed; the lights were off. I looked into the bathroom mirror. My eyes appeared squinty and drugged, my face plump and shiny, and my hair dirty and scraggly. Juliet—the girl with braids and a garland of flowers in her hair, wearing a white, silky dress—had disappeared. Maybe forever.

10

THREE weeks had passed. I was working at Mr. Wheatley's and back at school. After our fight I figured Vanessa would form her own "Parent Abuse" center, but instead of kicking me out or punishing me, she appeared at my door the next day and said, "Have it your way—work for Mr. Wheatley. Maybe it will do you some good."

And that was that. Even when I take three helpings of Wonder Bread at dinner, she keeps her mouth shut. Yet she still leaves clippings on my bed. Yesterday I found an article from *Reader's Digest:* "Cursory Remarks on Corpulence," or "You Can Kick That Fat Habit." She underlined "habit." I left a poem by Ogden Nash on her pillow:

> So I think it is very nice for ladies
> to be lithe and lissome.
> But not so much so that you cut yourself
> if you happen to embrace or kissome.

Vanessa and I engaged in a silent battle. With every bite of food I took, I knew I was the loser, but I couldn't stop. Why should I starve myself for her?

We hardly saw each other any more because I was either

working at the Health Food Store or rehearsing for *Romeo and Juliet*. By now I'd gained back all the weight I lost. Back to wearing layers of clothing. Underneath, layers and layers of fat were forming—my cushion against the world.

Mr. Wuensche, to whom I barely spoke any more, made one revealing comment: "We'll stuff your costume with pillows to make you look like the fat old Nurse."

Who was he kidding? I didn't need pillows to look like the fat old Nurse. I was already there. He must have been feeling badly for not giving me Juliet's part. But that remark made me even angrier. I promised to work on this play, but afterward Mr. Wuensche and his Drama Guild could be locked into a space capsule and shot to the moon for all I cared.

Nothing was going right at rehearsals, and Wuensche was showing definite signs of wear. The play was long, the lines difficult, and the cast uncooperative. No one wanted to sit down and talk about the implications of the story.

"This feels too much like English class," muttered John Levy, who played Mercutio.

And some of the lines were so overtly erotic that we all reacted with embarrassed giggles. When the boys practiced the dueling scenes, they fell all over each other, scuffling with uncontrollable rowdiness. Mainly because no one wanted to deal with the whole problem of two adolescents falling madly in love and committing suicide.

"Heavy, too heavy for me," John Levy muttered. Bensinger's voice box was hoarse from overexertion, as he croaked and coaxed us into behaving, into taking seriously what was too serious to be taken seriously.

But my main gripe was with Maude St. James. She may have looked like Juliet with her alabaster skin and innocent face (okay, her slender body as well) but her voice, even with the refined British accent, was cold, even haughty. She announced her lines as if she were a newscaster. "Two men robbed a bank, three people shot, and isn't it a lovely day?" No change in expression. She had not learned her part, even in the first act, in which she only had about ten short lines. And where were her symptoms of suffering? Why wasn't she exhibiting the vulnerability of a young girl caught in an ill-fated love affair? She needed lessons from me. More than anyone in the cast, in High Ridge, in the whole world, I wanted to play that part. Will the real Juliet please stand? I shouted to myself, imagining applause as I rose.

A star-crossed lover Maude was not. She moved across the stage like an ice princess in cool, measured steps, her stance regal, her voice crisp and domineering.

"What satisfaction canst thou have tonight?" she barked at David as if she were Queen Victoria instead of a guileless schoolgirl. I know what would satisfy me—watching Maude St. James fall off her self-erected balcony.

Yet David was perfect, following her in a love-sick-calf trot. If she had carried herself like glass, as if she were breakable, her portrayal of Juliet might have worked. But snow queens do not melt, and even David couldn't thaw her. I would have liked to banish her to the North Pole. But David was so urgently committed to the play and to Maude, as well (which I pretended was just his way of getting into his role) that I felt an obligation to help. One day I suggested we videotape the balcony scene so Maude and David could see how they looked. Maybe if she realized how badly she was coming across, she'd be able to improve.

Wuensche told me he was grateful for the suggestion. I didn't bother to say you're welcome. He continuously pulled his beard and shook his head, as if he'd made some huge error that couldn't be corrected. Call the whole thing off, I wanted to tell him, but as the old saying goes, you make your bed, you have to lie in it. The parents of High Ridge might burn down the Little Theater after this production.

"Gather around, folks," I called. "Let's watch this scene over the monitor." Concentrating intently for the first time, Maude was riveted to the set. Maybe there was hope for her. I wasn't sure I'd like her to succeed, but still I wanted to get my point across. At the place on the tape when she flubbed her lines and began improvising nervously, Maude let the group in on what she was really thinking.

"Why that's adorable, adorable," she gushed.

"That's not adorable," I blasted. "Adorable would be if you'd stop ad-libbing and memorize your lines."

Maude clicked off the video machine. Pointing an accusing finger at me, she yelled, "Get her out of here. I can't rehearse with that beast in here, watching every move I make, crunching on potato chips each time I rehearse with David."

Robert Bensinger, who was hovering nearby, trying to look like a director, bobbed up and down. He fluttered his arms like a startled bird. "Well now, well now. Maybe you'd just better leave for a while, Jodie . . ."

"I won't work until she's gone," stated Maude. "In fact, it's bloody impossible to work with her plodding around, criticizing me, glaring at me." Maude sank dramatically into a chair with her arms folded, her back to me.

I stood there ashamed, so incredulous that I couldn't budge. The rest of the kids were staring at me with hostility, as if it were all my fault that the play wasn't going well. Burning with anger, I fought back tears as David gently took my arm.

"Come on, Jodie. Let's take a soda break." Gratefully, I let him lead me down the aisle as I pulled my old poncho on and bowed my head so no one could see my face.

"David, you come back here this minute," screamed Maude, "as soon as you get rid of her."

"I don't know what's happening," David said, "but I have to go back. Maude is really falling apart. She needs me."

What about me, I wanted to ask? What about me? Just because I'm fat and don't look fragile doesn't mean I'm not falling apart.

"The cast will get over this," David was saying. "Everyone is just nervous. You're doing a great job. You've helped a lot."

"Apparently Maude doesn't feel that way. I'm not coming back."

"Look. I'll speak with her. She's under a lot of pressure— a new home, a new school, trying to prove herself. She has an artistic temperament. You don't know her the way I do," he said reverently. "She reminds me of one of those Greek maidens on the Erechtheion—graceful, innocent—"

"And on a pedestal?" I said crossly.

"I have to get back in there, Jodie," David repeated, squeezing my hand. "Tomorrow everything will be fine."

"Maybe for you," I said, but he was already dashing back to his Juliet. "Love goes toward love, as schoolboys from their books." And I—"love from love, toward school with heavy looks." Pulling a bag of potato chips out of my rucksack and crunching loudly, I pretended I was chewing right in Maude St. James's ear. Almost time for work, my only sanctuary now from the misery of my life in High Ridge. As for *Romeo and Juliet*, my contract had just been revoked and I was relieved to be out.

II

I DIDN'T want to burden Mr. Wheatley with my problems. In fact, working with him was such a cheering experience, I felt as if I should forget my troubles whenever I entered the Health Food Store. But after what just transpired at rehearsal, it wasn't easy to prance through the door like Shirley Temple singing "On the Good Ship Lollipop." After feebly attempting to smile in his direction, I tried to blare a hearty hello, but the sound that came forth resembled the squeaky chirp of a hungry bird. I immediately busied myself behind the counter mixing a batch of homemade yogurt. Soon, without even realizing it, I was slurping down more yogurt than was being dished into the container.

"Jodie, what are you doing?" Mr. Wheatley finally asked. "I don't mean to be nosy. Folks have a right to privacy, but you look as if something's bothering you today." He pretended not to notice the creamy remains of my dairy debacle. I looked away, afraid I might start crying.

"Jodie, Jodie. Working behind this counter all these years, I've heard my share of sad tales. And I've discovered that just talking about a problem sometimes makes it easier

68

to bear." He tipped my chin up so I had to look at him. "Now, don't I have a trustworthy face?" He puckered his lips like a kissing gourami, which caused me to laugh in spite of myself. Then he tiptoed to the front door as if trying to sneak off without being noticed, flipped the BACK IN FIVE MINUTES sign around, drew the curtain, and motioned me over to one of the booths. "I guess all the health nuts outside ready to bang the door down for my magical bran flakes can wait a few minutes." I laughed again. No one was outside. He resembled a mischievous pixie creeping across the room. What a nice man! He was not being kind to me out of pity, like David. There are some things that I sense instinctively. I knew I could trust him.

"I was thrown out of *Romeo and Juliet* rehearsal today," I began after we were settled into a booth sipping on hot jasmine tea. "The leading lady had a fit when I pointed out her inadequacies." I tried to tell my story with indignant pride, but soon, with Mr. Wheatley's gentle prodding and sympathetic nods, I sniffled and blurted out everything. After what seemed like a long speech on the injustice of it all, I whispered, "And my mother's driving me crazy. Sometimes I hate her."

I'd never said that aloud to another living soul, not even to Heather. Maybe I was ashamed because Heather loved her parents so much, and admitting I hated Vanessa would shock her. But Mr. Wheatley didn't act shocked. In fact, he was sympathetic. "And how do you feel about yourself?"

"It's horrible being a fat, ugly wad. I hate myself, too, but when my mother nags, I go on an eating binge just to spite her."

"Sounds like a vicious circle," said Mr. Wheatley. "Eat-

69

ing is your only weapon against her. It's natural to want to fight back if someone tries to overpower you. But your way of fighting back does you more harm than good."

"That's for sure," I said. "If things don't get better, I'll end up weighing three hundred pounds."

"Well, you can't hold your mother responsible for that," he remarked, raising one bushy eyebrow. "Mothers can be a problem, I'll grant you that. My mother was so tough she could scare the spots off a leopard. In fact, I ran away from home when I was sixteen. Only went back years later when I could bring Mrs. Wheatley along for moral support. But I had to set things right before it was too late. I remember Mother sitting on the front porch as I stood there, squeezing Mrs. Wheatley's hand, while I tried to erase all those silent, angry years that stood between us."

"Better than all the noisy, angry years I've had with Vanessa," I murmured.

"Sometimes I wonder, if I had stayed, if we could have reached an agreement. I knew my mother didn't understand what all I was trying to say that day, but somehow she was glad I came back. We had a bowl of soup together."

"Did you have trouble talking to her?" My discussions with Vanessa never varied. The rhythm was always the same, discordant, convoluted.

"I can't say it wasn't uncomfortable. She never said the things I longed to be told when I was a lonely, henpecked little boy, but still . . ." A sad, faraway look came into his eyes as he said, "Things don't always turn out the way they should. But no one, not my mother or anyone else, could make me give up my dreams. Like the poet Langston Hughes said, 'Hold fast to dreams.' "

I was about to confide my plan to run away when Mr. Wheatley popped up, leaping to the center of the floor. "Now, enough of my long, sad tales, our long, sad faces. Jodie, you're the entertainer. Entertain me. Tell me a story with a happy ending."

I wasn't sure I wanted to play. "I don't know any real life stories with happy endings, just fairy tales."

"Well, then, tell me a fairy tale. What was your favorite story when you were a little girl?" He propped himself up on the counter, crossed his short legs, and peered at me expectantly. "Center stage. You're on." He used such exuberant cajolery that I couldn't help trying to please him.

"Well, I do remember one story that I loved."

"Out with it," he shouted.

"I used to make my mother tell it to me over and over." I took a deep, dramatic breath and began. "Once there was a fat little prince. He was spoiled rotten and a terrible glutton. But everything the prince wanted his doting parents provided. He had rooms piled high with toys, closets full of clothes, and live entertainment every night before he went to bed. He gobbled up molasses bars, fudge, tarts, and whole roasts faster than the royal chef could cook them. The palace was in a continual state of frantic activity trying to satisfy his increasingly outlandish demands. One day he called in the royal chef and said, 'I want a dish that is cold as winter and hot as summer at the same time.' The king and queen nodded indulgently. But no matter what the chef concocted, he could not create such a dish. Chefs from all over the world were brought in, but no one succeeded in inventing a recipe that was both hot as summer and cold as winter at the same time. The royal brat threw royal

71

tantrums. His royal parents were beside themselves with royal dismay. —So how do you like it so far?" I asked Mr. Wheatley.

"Go on. Go on. Your mother sure picked a dilly of a story to tell you."

"Well, to make a long story short," I concluded, noticing a few customers at the door, "one day an old woman from the village, dressed in rags, appeared at the palace gate. She had heard of the prince's passion and claimed she had the perfect recipe. The chef was so desperate that he let her enter. That night the pork-out prince banged his chubby fists on the table. To the sound of trumpets, the peasant woman entered carrying a huge covered silver tray. And lo and behold! When the prince snatched up the lid, he found what he had been waiting for, a dish that was hot as summer and cold as winter at the same time." I paused dramatically.

"Good heavens, what was it?" cried Mr. Wheatley.

Grinning devilishly, I announced, "A HOT FUDGE SUNDAE."

"Now there's the first fairy tale I've ever heard that has no redeeming value to it whatsoever," snorted Mr. Wheatley. "Why, that's downright outrageous! You must be leaving some piece out."

"Not at all," I told him. "The moral of the story is that it's possible to come up with the impossible." Mr. Wheatley started to comment, but changed his mind as he toddled over to unlock the door. But I knew what he was thinking. And he was right. Hot fudge sundaes wouldn't make that spoiled prince happy. He'd just think of something else he wanted. There's no one who deserves everything; and no one can have it both ways, especially me.

12

Monday morning the school secretary handed me a note. "Please come see me during your free period. Albert Wuensche." I wondered what he wanted. After all, I had dropped out of the play.

My first class was English. We were reading Dickens's *Pickwick Papers*. The only empty chair was next to the elephant lady, Wanda Sue Weatherly, who smiled at me as if we were soul sisters. I squeezed into my seat without acknowledging her.

Miss Whiting began to lecture on the genius of Dickens, his mastery of vivid description. I hadn't read the assignments, so I took her word for it.

"Consider his images in delineating the character of Joe, the Fat Boy." As she prepared to read a passage, I prepared to tune out, but the first line leaped off the page; Miss Whiting's husky voice commanded my attention.

" 'Sundry taps on his head with a stick and the fat boy with some difficulty roused from his lethargy. 'Come, hand in the eatables!'

" 'There was something in the sound of the last word which aroused the unctuous boy. He jumped up; and the

73

leaden eyes, which twinkled behind his mountainous cheeks, leered horribly upon the food as he unpacked it from the basket.

" 'Now, make haste,' said Mr. Wardle, for the fat boy was hanging fondly over a capon, which he seemed wholely unable to part with. The boy sighed deeply, and bestowing an ardent gaze upon its plumpness, unwillingly consigned it to his master.' "

Suddenly it seemed that every face in the classroom was directed toward me and Wanda Sue. Obviously there was no way I could look at Wanda, who heaved a sigh. I stared defiantly at the taunting grins, at Miss Whiting, who was flipping pages and talking very rapidly. Then, mortified, I buried my head in the text. Miss Whiting continued her speech on the marvels of English literature. The rest of the class period passed so slowly that I considered trying to sneak out. Perspiring profusely under my heavy sweater and poncho, I rejoiced when the bell finally rang, and scurried to the exit. Wanda Sue was right behind me.

"Jodie," she said, tapping me on the shoulder, "may I speak with you for a minute?" Abruptly I swung around.

"I'm really in a big hurry." For the first time I forced myself to look at her face, which was surprisingly fresh and pretty, despite the double chin. She had a sweet smile, so unthreatening that I couldn't refuse the request. "Well, just for a minute," I mumbled crossly. Not wanting to be seen with Wanda, I trailed behind, following her broad back into the student lounge. With snide satisfaction, I noted that I was not as fat as she, but I couldn't help noticing that she was dressed neatly in a soft blue smock dress, her curly hair clean and well kempt. She sank heavily into a corner chair.

"That was quite a passage Miss Whiting chose to read. Rather insensitive of her, don't you think?"

I nodded.

"Every time she used the word *fat*, I squirmed," she continued. "You must have been feeling the same way."

I don't want to be identified with you, I'm thinking. Don't single me out to be your cohort. Several girls walked by and waved to Wanda, who shouted back a hearty greeting. What a surprise to find she had friends. "So what are you trying to tell me?" I asked. "That being fat, ridiculed, and ostracized by society is no fun? I already know that."

"I don't feel ostracized, Jodie," replied Wanda. "If people don't like me because I'm fat, that's their problem."

"You don't enjoy being *fat*," I demanded in disbelief, "do you?"

"Not particularly; but I can never be thin, so I've learned to accept myself. I'm not unhealthy or lethargic like Dickens's Joe, and I don't feel uncomfortable just because I'm heavy."

"Well, nobody's born to be fat," I said nastily. "It makes me uncomfortable."

"I know I'm not a raving beauty," said Wanda. "But who needs to be a raving beauty?"

"Well I don't want to be a candidate for life membership at the fat farm, either," I retorted.

"So why don't you lose weight instead of feeling sorry for yourself?"

"It's not so easy. Every time I start a diet, I get upset and blow it."

"I'm so far gone now," said Wanda, "I need major

surgery to get rid of my flab." Something about the way she said "major surgery" made me giggle. We both started giggling, but I felt teary at the same time.

Then, despite myself, I confessed, "I feel awful all the time. I can't stop eating."

"It's funny how one pretzel turns into twenty; it makes me shudder to think of all the homemade loaves of bread I've eaten with the idea of taking just one slice. But my mother is such a terrific cook. She piles it on every night. You should see my brother, Louie. Our whole family is enormous." Wanda Sue shook her head helplessly, as if gluttony were a hereditary disease.

"My mother rarely cooks. Her idea of a nourishing meal is a cup of yogurt. She's a string-bean worshipper and never lets me forget I look like an eggplant."

"Maybe food isn't your problem," she offered. "Maybe it's your mother."

That was certainly not a new insight, I thought, but I found myself saying, "No, I'm the problem."

Wanda Sue leaned over and engulfed me in a big, cuddly hug. For a second I froze, then found myself squeezing her back.

"You're going to be okay," she said. "But you've got to get rid of that silly poncho. You're not that heavy. It looks like a tent."

"Okay, okay. I promise." I laughed. "I'm sick of it myself. And thanks." I hadn't said "thank you" to anyone for weeks, not even to Mr. Wheatley. Thank you—the words felt good, and so did the hug. My mother was wrong. Just because someone was overweight didn't mean she was disgusting or unlovable. What I saw before me was a nice girl, who joked about being fat. On another level, Wanda

Sue was saying, "It's no fun being fat, but I'm stuck with it and so I might as well get used to it."

But I didn't want to get used to being fat, whatever that meant. I wasn't so far gone that I needed major surgery, and, in my case, it certainly wasn't hereditary. Now there was a new insight, I realized as I headed for Mr. Wuensche's office.

Somehow I was not nervous about seeing him. What went on at rehearsal wasn't my fault, no matter how the rest of the cast felt.

Mr. Wuensche was slumped over his desk, which was covered with scripts and papers. He motioned me to sit down. "Listen to this," he said plaintively, reading from a volume of criticism. " 'The role of Juliet has been performed successfully only by a handful of actresses, all mature women, experienced *grandes dames* of the theater. The complexity of the role has never been believably portrayed by a thirteen-year-old nymphet; yet the audience fully accepts Shakespeare's notion that a pubescent girl is capable of grandiloquent, impassioned emotions, and that the tragic outcome is indeed possible. Renditions of Shakespeare's *Romeo and Juliet* are more satisfactory when adapted for ballet or the opera.' " He leaned back, exhaling a long, ponderous sigh. "There is not a high school drama teacher in the country who would attempt to do this play. How could I have deluded myself?"

"Maybe the whole thing will pull together," I offered weakly. "Maybe you can cut some of the scenes."

"No," he said. "I will not present a slipshod, ill-constructed exhibition."

"How about turning it into a reader's theater? Everyone can stand in a line and read their parts."

Mr. Wuensche was actually looking to me for advice, instead of booting me out. His lips were twitching as he pulled on his beard in befuddlement. I wondered if he was afraid of losing his job, or if he was sincerely devoted to art.

"I really love you kids," he said sadly. "I don't want to let you down." I couldn't be much lower, but in the spirit of 'Don't hit a man when he's down,' I tried to play a supportive role. I have to admit to feeling some empathic twinges for Mr. Wuensche; he was in bad shape.

"Jodie, I need you to hear me out," Mr. Wuensche continued. "Yes, I am an English teacher, but I don't consider Drama Guild a hobby. The plays we present are the only live theater that most of our audience ever sees. Football games, movies, and car races are more interesting to people in this town than the theater. But I love doing these productions, and that's enough reason to do them."

"But why did you choose such a difficult play?" I couldn't help asking him. "You know the situation in this school."

"Oh, I realize they want me to put on sure-fire popular stuff, like *Charlie Brown* or *Oklahoma!* Popularity is an American religion. But I think you all deserve better."

"What do you want me to do? I'm not exactly a favorite with the group any more."

"That's not true. The cast is suffering from low morale and they had to take it out on someone. After you left the other day, several people said they were sorry. They asked me to speak with you. I was about to come after you right then and there, but Maude began sobbing and I had to calm her down."

A disgusted smirk spread over my face. I can never be sympathetic toward Maude St. James.

"I know, I know," he said. "She's very difficult. Please

give us another chance. Maybe we can salvage this disaster after all if we work together."

I wanted to offer him some hope, but I felt as discouraged as he did. Nevertheless, I promised to return to rehearsals.

"I'm relieved to hear you say that. You're a good kid, Jodie."

I knew I should take that as a compliment, but I didn't want to be considered a "good kid." I wanted more for myself. It was as if there were some strange inner drama going on linking me to David, Maude, and Mr. Wuensche. Where it was all leading to, what the conclusion would be, I didn't have any idea. What a strange day! My mind was swirling, as if I were playing a dissonant symphony in my head. Elbowing past the crowd of students mingling in front of the Coke machines, I loped into the cafeteria. In a haphazard arrangement, a pile of sandwiches, potato chips, and custard found its way to my tray, and I wasn't even hungry.

Dumping the unopened food in the trash container, I decided to break my boycott of the library and hide out there until next period. Maybe I could find some answers in the card catalogue under *confusion*.

13

I was surprised to find Vanessa home from Trumbells already. Only four o'clock. Myrna was sitting next to her on the couch. Vanessa was sobbing; Myrna, moaning.

"Men," she groaned. "You can't trust them further than you can throw them." Myrna has a way with words.

"Barney's the first man I've opened up to since Sam died," wailed Vanessa. "How could he have treated me so badly?" I'd never heard my mother mention my father's name in a positive way.

"Men are beasts," said Myrna.

"This time I thought I was doing everything right. I sympathized with his complaints about his ex-wife. I took an interest in his rotten, pimply-faced son; I cooked meals for him, even cleaned his apartment last week. And now he tells me he can't make a commitment, that I'm too demanding, that I remind him of his mother." Barney's mother must be a real case if she was anything like Vanessa.

I turned toward my own room, but Vanessa said, "Jodie, stay here. You might as well listen to this." I sank into the armchair. I was hungry and eyed the bowl of unsalted cashews.

"I've called him a hundred times, but his secretary tells me he's in a meeting or out of the office. Why doesn't he have the decency to confront me? How was I so stupid to become involved again?" She grabbed Myrna's arm. "I should have listened to you, Myrna. You were right about him. He's a cad."

"I was never taken in by that slow, seductive drawl," Myrna said with a hint of satisfaction. "He was just playing games with you, trying to see how far he could get." Queen Jargonella should be writing dialogue for *True Confessions*.

"How is it possible for a man to be so warm one minute and cold the next? We made plans, promises, but he refuses to come through for me." Usually Vanessa only got this upset over me. It was almost a relief to have her fixating on someone else for a change. I even felt angry for her. Our household was being plagued by rejections.

"It sounds as if he's frightened, Mother," I told her. "You come on so strong sometimes."

She cocked her head and regarded me with her raised-eyebrow look. "What do you mean by that?"

"You always act so sure of yourself, as if you don't need to rely on anyone. David Simms thinks I'm tough, too; so he doesn't bother worrying that I may be suffering inside."

"David Simms? What about David Simms? What's been going on between you and that Simms boy?" Any mention of him or any of the Simms family and she got huffy.

"Nothing," I answered. "I had a bad time in rehearsal the other day and he didn't understand, and I was afraid to tell him what I really felt."

"That's the problem," sighed Vanessa. "I finally admitted to Barney how I felt and he ran the other way. Said he was being swallowed alive; I was pushing him too soon. I'm just not a patient, shrinking violet. I wanted immediate satisfaction. All right, I even thought about marriage."

"Well, there's nothing wrong with asking for what you want," came Myrna's indignant voice. "You didn't do anything wrong. He must be used to a different kind of woman." I couldn't help but agree with that. Vanessa's not the picture of the passive wife and mother. She's a different species altogether. I don't want to be like her, but I don't want to be like the other, either.

There I was sitting around with my mother and Myrna, talking girl talk—a participant in the conversation instead of an outsider, and for the first time in my life I could understand what my mother was going through.

"I just can't take all of this responsibility any more. I'm tired of depending on myself." Vanessa began crying again in broken, hiccupy sobs.

"So who doesn't need to be taken care of once in a while?" Myrna asked. "You just picked the wrong person. At least you tried to have a relationship. That's a start. The next time will be better."

"Look at it this way," I told Vanessa. "You took three steps forward and one backward."

"I feel as if all my defenses are down, that the barriers I've set up all these years have been smashed. I hated exposing myself. I feel like going over to his place, banging on the windows, and challenging him to a duel." Vanessa was perking up. A revenge fantasy always does the trick.

"Now you're talking," said Myrna. "Let's all go over there."

"We can dress up in costume and serenade him," I

offered. Some of the old defiance came into Vanessa's expression. She even sneered her old familiar sneer.

"I guess it's not the end of the world, but he was sure nice to snuggle with. I'd forgotten how it felt."

"You want to snuggle," said Myrna. "Then we'll snuggle. Get over here, Jodie." So the three of us clasped arms around each other.

"It's not the same," remarked Vanessa, "but it helps."

We cuddled together on the couch in silence. Three misfits lumped together, a blend of odors—tobacco, perfume, perspiration—we clung to each other, holding on. I was holding on to my mother! We had not touched affectionately in years; yet I'd always felt her insistent grasp, like an iron cuff, around my neck. It was a moment to savor because, for once, the bonds were not confining, just comforting.

Then Myrna said, "Vanessa, I have to confess something. I've been so jealous of you and Barney, I could hardly stand it. You're skinny, have a great job, a child, all the things I yearn for, and then you fall in love, too. I was miserable. When you told me you and Barney split up, I wanted to celebrate."

Vanessa bolted up. "I'm not sure I want to hear this, Myrna. First Barney, now even you, my best friend, are against me?"

"Wait a minute. Listen to me. Not against you, just jealous. My life is hardly a bed of roses, either." I was seeing Myrna Hochman with new eyes. The two women regarded each other stiffly.

"Look at us," Myrna said. "Going at it like two old crones. If we can't trust each other after all these years . . ."

"Then we're in big trouble," conceded Vanessa.

Relieved, I reached for the cashews. Mother glared at me. Some things never change. I stuffed a handful in my mouth and chomped with a scowl.

"Now, don't you start with me, Jodie," Vanessa screamed. "You're going to blow up like a balloon and pop if you keep doing that."

"So what?" I snarled. "It's not your problem." The unappealing wad again. I was again conscious of how repugnant she found me.

"It certainly is my problem. I've put up with this long enough." So it started: our moment of peace was over.

"Vanessa, will you cut this out," Myrna shouted. "The two of you are going to damage each other permanently, if you haven't already."

"Don't tell me how to be a mother," snapped Vanessa. "You have no idea what's been happening here."

"I know enough to tell you to leave this child alone. Look, we both have a vacation coming up. You're really on edge. I need a change of scenery, and so do you. Why don't we take off for a few weeks, take a cruise, go to a resort . . . Club Med, that's an idea. I saw an ad in the *Times*. They're offering a two-week special." Myrna to the rescue. Her rapid, insistent speech shut Vanessa up for a minute.

"What will I do about Jodie? I can't just traipse off and leave her in this place alone."

"Well, I'm certainly not going with you," I snorted. Vanessa paced. Myrna smoked a cigarette. I glowered at both of them and chewed on cashews.

"I could use a few weeks away," admitted Vanessa. "I need time to think, to get over Barney. Oh, to get some sun, to get out of this dreary town." My sentiments exactly.

Summoning all my courage, I said, "I have a suggestion. Why don't I stay with someone while you two take off?"

"Who? Who could you stay with?" Vanessa was verging on belligerence again. I knew enough to keep quiet. Let her figure it out. Maybe there was a maiden aunt to dump me on.

"I have only one relative within fifty miles," said Vanessa, "and he would hardly be the proper chaperone for Jodie."

"Jodie has friends. Surely she can find someone," suggested Myrna. "You can trust her. I'm dying to go to the Caribbean. I can hear the steel guitars already." She did a quick cha-cha and snapped her fingers. We both regarded Vanessa hopefully.

"Let me think about it. Right now I need a shower and a good night's sleep." Myrna and I were dismissed.

"Think hard," instructed Myrna, wrapping herself in rabbit fur and unlocking the front door. "All I need is my bikini and airline ticket, and I'm ready to fly South for the winter." Fly away, fly away, I pleaded silently.

That night I imagined a flock of sea gulls circling above a turquoise sea. In the lead were two large white birds, decorated in beads and glitter, with strangely familiar faces. A plump little gull was flying in the other direction. The mother bird gave a high-pitched, shrill caw for the baby to get back in line. The little gull floundered, spinning in mid-air amid the shrieking din; then gradually gained its own momentum and flew away.

14

ARMED with her bikini, plane ticket, Myrna, and four pieces of pink Samsonite, Vanessa flew off to sandy beaches and sky-blue waters. Overwhelmed by visions of romance and adventure on tropical shores (with Myrna's vociferous prodding), she grudgingly allowed me to stay with the Simmses. For once I was grateful for Myrna's unflagging persistence. When David offered to give them a lift to the airport, she even agreed to that. In fact, all week her major attitude had been "agreeable." I restrained myself until her plane was out of sight.

"Free at last!" I yelled as Heather, David, and I raced out of the airport, cheering and shaking the hands of bewildered travelers in our path. Heather, who toted her baton even to the bathroom, did a double-looped toss, flipping the stick so high I thought it might be caught in the jet stream of Vanessa's plane.

Piling into David's Jeep, we sang in raucous harmony all the way back to High Ridge. I was glad to see David in such good spirits; he'd been moping lately, presumably discouraged about the play and Maude St. James. My move to the Simmses' would provide a chance to work with him on the script and to offer some needed encouragement. Practicing Juliet's lines with David was better than nothing.

Snow fell in steady, white streams, coating the trees and buildings of High Ridge like frosting on a cake. Whitewashed, the town's drab surface was hidden. A fresh snowfall, another fresh start for me.

With gravel flying, David swerved the Jeep into the garage. Small or large, his movements fascinated me: the way he jingled the car keys in his hand, just to hear the sound, before he tucked them carefully under the floor mat and reached down to pick up any discarded papers; the way he swung Heather out of the seat and swirled her, shouting, "I'm crazy about snow. I've been waiting for it. Time to haul out my easel and paint that elm." As if dressed in white armor, the tree stood guard over the barn. And David, my white knight, threw his arms around the trunk, calling, "Jodie, have you hugged a tree today?"

"His mood is improving," whispered Heather. "That Maude St. James! All those frantic phone calls. Then suddenly she appears at our door, whispers with David, and leaves in a huff. Poor David is so confused, he's behaving erratically. His mood fluctuates like a thermometer." Erratic behavior. I was an expert on the subject.

"I hope she doesn't show up while I'm here. Although I'm so happy to be out of that apartment and staying with you that the whole British Army could be camped on your doorstep and I wouldn't care."

"The whole British Army?" said Heather, her eyes narrowing. "Now, that sounds interesting! Entertaining the troops?"

"Right. You could twirl your baton. I could recite Shakespeare."

"Soup's on, you ruffians," Mr. Simms called from the porch. "Good heavens, Jodie, I thought we'd have to kidnap you or at least sign a release statement to convince your mother of this visitation." He wrapped me in his arms, patting my back. I hugged him back, close to tears again.

"We welcome you to Camp Simms," he boomed. "We're awfully glad you're here."

"We'll set the air reverberating with a mighty cheer," chimed in Mrs. Simms, motioning us in out of the cold. Traipsing behind us, David and Heather joined in. "We'll sing you in; we'll sing you out. For you we'll give a mighty shout. Hail, hail the gang's all here and you're welcome to our menagerie."

Laughing and crying now, I blubbered, "You don't need to make a fuss over me."

"Of course we do," said Mrs. Simms. "You're one of the family now. A cause for celebration." I looked at their faces and knew they were happy I was there. If they pitied me, if they thought I was fat and ugly, someone to feel sorry for, they didn't show it. And I felt part of the family. For once I wasn't lonely or sad. Please, I prayed, please let this last.

"Lord, bless this house that it shall be filled with love, safe and sound in harmony." After grace, we settled around the long refectory table with Mr. Simms at the head. Every now and then he jumped up to help his wife, or to throw another log in the open hearth as he directed the conversation, gently drawing me out. He was like the host of *The Canterbury Tales*, rewarding us for the best story with his

88

approving laughter. Is this the end or the beginning of a journey? I wondered. The setting reminded me of a country inn, all of us jolly travelers. A stopping place, a starting place? I wasn't sure which.

For a girl to whom paper plates, plastic flowers, and TV dinners were a way of life, a sit-down meal with flowered china, crystal goblets, and sterling silverware on lace doilies was not only "wondrous strange," as Mr. Shakespeare said, but awe-inspiring. A centerpiece of fresh yellow mums nodded gaily from a woven straw basket; tall white candles gleamed in the brass candelabra. A Beethoven sonata for piano and violin played in the background. All these details filled me with such a sense of well-being that I found myself chattering to Mr. and Mrs. Simms, David, Heather, and even Plato, the cat, in a delirium of run-on sentences, punctuated with exclamation points. Mrs. Simms fluttered in and out carrying platters of fresh carrots and asparagus, a wooden salad bowl filled with lettuce and tomatoes, and a steaming hot peach compote. I loved the meal and her. A small, plump figure clad in a full gray skirt and white apron, she reminded me of a pigeon. She hopped in quick rhythms, always concerned with keeping her brood happy.

Mr. Simms, Heather, and David thrived in this atmosphere created by Mrs. Simms's nesting instincts. Even Plato purred in lazy contentment by the fire. Vanessa might sniff and call Mrs. Simms dowdy, but in her presence I could relax. She made domesticity look so appealing that I offered to do the dishes.

"I'll dry," volunteered David, which conjured up an image of me standing over the sink, gazing into his eyes through a mountain of soap suds. The telephone's sharp ring brought me out of my daydream and David up from the table. Almost toppling the chair down in his haste, he took the call in the kitchen.

The family exchanged concerned glances.

"Maude again," sighed Heather. "David may be in for another siege."

"The British are coming. Hurrah! Hurrah!" sang Mr. Simms tonelessly.

"Now, don't say anything," warned Mrs. Simms. "This Maude business is becoming his Achilles' heel."

We overheard David's impatient "But, Maude," three times and then a loud clunk.

"He either kicked the wall or hung up on her," remarked Heather.

"Hush, now." Mrs. Simms put her finger to her lips. Clearly distraught, David slumped back to his chair, eyes downcast.

Mr. Simms cleared his throat. "I usually don't suggest this after such a fine meal, but we ought to let Jodie in on an old family custom. Every now and then we hold a powwow. Each of us has a turn to register a complaint, to air any grievances that we may have." He turned to me. "It gives us an opportunity to squawk out loud instead of carrying excess baggage around in our heads."

"Excess baggage," remarked Heather dryly, "is a term Father picked up when TWA charged him for overweight."

"Not at all," protested Mr. Simms. "There was an article in *Psychology Today*."

"What was it called?" asked David. " 'Psycho Babble'?" Banter, exchanged affectionately, so unlike the sarcasm Vanessa and I usually engaged in.

Yet there was a hint of tension. Not wanting to spoil a perfect evening, I quickly announced, "Well, I, for one, have no complaints whatsoever. This is the nicest meal I've ever had."

"Thank you," Mrs. Simms said happily. "I hope you didn't mind that we served no meat or starch. I've eliminated them from my menu planning."

"Frankly, if you haven't noticed, I don't need that kind of food." I laughed, free to joke about my weight for a change. Mrs. Simms looked relieved.

David spoke up. "As long as Jodie's here and directly involved with my problem, I might as well spill it." Although we all knew what he was referring to, nobody made a big deal out of his pronouncement; no one pressured him. "This play at school is becoming a farce. I've never been involved in such a calamity. We're demolishing Shakespeare. It's like putting his script in a paper shredder. The words come out stripped of their meaning. The worst of it is that Maude can't memorize her lines. I've tried writing cues on her hands, in cards tucked under her sleeve. I've hidden copies of her long speeches all over the set. I test, tease, repeat, but nothing works. She's so flustered that she yells at me and starts crying."

The solution I wanted to offer was trading her in for a new Juliet, but I restrained myself.

"Aren't you taking a lot of responsibility on yourself?" Mr. Simms asked. "You're making her problem into your problem."

"Maude should talk to Mr. Wuensche," Heather said. "He's the director, not you."

Shaking his head, David answered, "I'm the one

responsible. I convinced her to audition. I thought she'd be perfect. She's trying. I see her struggling, and it's all my fault."

"Sounds like the young lady knows how to play on a young man's sympathy," Mr. Simms said.

"Now she's furious and hung up on me. I wish I'd never gotten involved with this stupid play."

I was responsible for that, I thought.

"You're not Sir Galahad," said Heather. "You can't spend your life saving damsels in distress."

"I feel more like Don Quixote chasing windmills." David shrugged.

"Now's the time to concentrate your energy on the play, not on that girl," said Mr. Simms. "All you can do is try, give it your best shot."

Thrusting his chair back, David crumpled his lace-edged napkin and pitched it on the table. "Oh, right, Father—my best shot. When you see me on stage, you'll have a fit. Then you can give me your famous lecture on quality versus mediocrity."

"Look, son. I don't expect everything you do to be perfect—"

"Sure, sure," retorted David.

"Listen," I broke in, "Wuensche realizes there are pitfalls with this production. If it doesn't get any better, he'll postpone the opening."

"I'm not a quitter," David said stubbornly.

"That's not the point," said Heather, but she chose not to continue. No one wanted to embarrass David into admitting the real issue. If Mr. Simms realized that David was hung up on Maude, he didn't show it. It occurred to me that maybe he couldn't understand how David felt. In his own way, Mr. Simms was just as dense about his son as Vanessa was about me.

Roughly, David heaved a log on the fire. As the flame crackled and sparks flew, he stalked out.

Mr. Simms started to follow, but Mrs. Simms put her finger to her lips again. Obviously she knew what was going on.

"Father, let him alone. The play and Maude's inability to memorize her lines are not his only excess baggage."

The excess baggage is Maude St. James, I thought bitterly, as smoke hissed in assent from the fireplace. He's in love with the wrong Juliet.

15

AFTER ten days of fresh vegetables and salads at the Simmses', plus Mr. Wheatley's sprout sandwiches, and two weeks of no Vanessa, I could tighten my belt two notches. Wanda Sue had convinced me to pitch my old plaid poncho, so I crept out of hibernation.

In fact, I was enjoying food and dieting at the same time. There were moments when I was tempted to take a second helping or sneak into the icebox, but no one cared whether I did or not, so I didn't.

However, last night I was roused by a nightmare. Shivering, I thought I was back in my cold bedroom. The dream was so vivid and terrible, it seemed real. We were giving the play before an audience. Whenever I spoke, someone from the shadows would scream, "Get off the stage." I couldn't see her face. No matter how loud I said my lines, the other voice drowned me out. Soon my mouth opened and closed but no sounds came out.

I lay in bed feeling scared and lonely for the first time in days. Tiptoeing past Heather's room, I saw she was asleep and didn't want to disturb her. I found myself creeping downstairs to the icebox, but when the door swung open, I realized it wasn't food I was craving. The empty feeling wasn't hunger. I needed someone to talk to, *not* Mrs. Simms's chocolate cream pie. As I reached in to pull out the platter anyway, a voice said, "No." Not Vanessa's or the screaming voice of my dream, but my own voice. I closed the door and went back to bed.

The next morning a bright-eyed girl with a wholesome, competent face stared at me from the mirror.

"Aren't you proud of yourself?" I asked the reflection. My face grinned back.

In the hall, I overheard Mr. Simms tell David, "Just do your best, that's all." This produced a grunt from David as he shuffled down the stairs.

"Jodie," called Mrs. Simms, "I forgot to give you this letter postmarked Martinique. Must be from your mother."

Gingerly I took the envelope and slowly tore open the flap. "Dear Jodie," began the note on rainbow stationery reeking of gardenias. Her handwriting was big and scrawling. "I have to hand it to Myrna. She was right. We're having a ball. You should see us, soaking up the sun all day. At night we wrap ourselves in flowered sarongs and dance to the music of steel guitars. Right now I'm swinging in a hammock under a thatched umbrella and sipping a piña colada. Myrna is dog-paddling back and forth in the kidney-shaped pool. She has her head above water to keep her hair dry."

From between the pages of the letter a Club Med newspaper clipping fell with a photo of Vanessa and Myrna—*WWD* style—in grass skirts slithering around a grinning beach boy. From the tone of the letter, Vanessa seemed in a good mood. Don't come home early, I told the letter.

"I've had plenty of time to think, to talk things over with

Myrna. We spend hours planning diabolical tricks to play on Mr. Kramer. We laugh a lot, even over our disasters with men. Although my relationship with Barney didn't work out, at least I tried. Taking this trip was the next step.

"But more important, I've been thinking about you and me. I'll admit I'm not the world's greatest mother. All those self-help books went in one ear and out the other. Bite your tongue, I tell myself every time we have a fight. But then I go ahead and open my big mouth. Myrna says my problem is called 'Hoof-in-Mouth' disease. It's just that I don't want you to make the mistakes I did and find yourself wondering if it's too late when you hit forty.

"Sometimes I get so frustrated, I take it out on you. A few days relaxing on the beach made me realize how cranky I've been. But you haven't been in such a good mood either. I found a good article in *Cosmopolitan*, 'The Art of Compromise.' I'll save it for you.

"Well, the social director is blowing his whistle. Volleyball time. I'm going to run in the other direction. Myrna will be right behind me, headed for the souvenir shop. Love, Mother.

"P.S. Are you thin yet?"

This line was crossed out but I could still read it.

"P.P.S. Last night Myrna and I won the Bingo jackpot. The prize was one more week at Club Med, which is an offer Myrna and I can't refuse. Hope the Simmses won't mind. See you soon."

Instead of throwing the letter away, I found myself rereading it. What surprised me was Vanessa's admitting she had made mistakes. Did she really mean it? Underneath the joking tone, my mother was making a serious peace offer. Still, I was glad she wasn't coming back yet. I don't know how long I sat there reading the letter over and over, before David's impatient voice startled me.

"Jodie, we're going to be late. Hurry up!"

"I'm coming," I shouted, racing outside to the garage to climb in David's Jeep.

"Don't forget your papaya juice," called Mrs. Simms.

I felt as if I'd just been acquitted, released, vindicated of a crime I didn't commit. Another ten days with the Simmses, and an unspoken promise from Vanessa that things between us would be different.

Mr. Wuensche had called an early meeting of the cast, so David and I were expected before classes. David's glum expression warned me into silence as he backed the Jeep out of the garage.

When he ran a stop sign, I gripped the seat and glanced over at his grim profile.

"Sorry," he muttered. Foul mood or not, I needed to tell him my news.

"Vanessa's staying in Martinique. She won't be back for another week."

"Great, that's great," he responded without much enthusiasm. "That's where I'd like to be right now, but I'd settle for New York."

"Only two hours by train," I mused. David's wish reminded me of my own plans, but I hadn't dreamed about going there since coming to the Simmses'.

"Someday I'll live in New York and spend every day at the Met. Park my easel in front of a Rembrandt or Hans Hofmann and paint all day."

"You mean you're giving up the theater?" I said in a half-serious voice.

"Doing this play makes me feel like a fish on land who

really wants to fly," remarked David. "Dad says I'm too much of a loner, that a group effort is good for me."

"Good for you?" I repeated. "You mean, like eating spinach?"

He laughed. "You're right. What a travesty! Tastes terrible, but it's going to make me big and strong. I'm committed to swallowing it even though I feel like throwing up every time I go to rehearsal. Besides the fact that Maude and I are constantly fighting, I don't even like acting."

"Why don't you quit?" I asked.

"I can't," he answered vehemently. "I'm not giving up." He clutched the steering wheel so tightly that his knuckles turned white.

At the Little Theater, the cast was assembled on stage. Maude planted herself on Juliet's bed, apart from the rest of us. David took his place beside her. She gave him a sullen look. Even pouting, she had the face of a porcelain doll.

Wuensche paced nervously; Bensinger, two steps behind, cleared his throat. "Mr. Wuensche and I have made some notes. I'll begin with Romeo. David, you keep missing your cues—"

"How can anybody know when to come in when Maude forgets her lines?" John Levy complained. Their voices gathered momentum as if they were doing fast dialogue in a script.

Maude: "There are too many bloody speeches to memorize . . ."

David: "We just need more practice . . ."

Me: "Why don't we divide into small groups . . ."

Bensinger: "Hold on, I'm not finished with David . . ."

David: "Lay off, Bensinger . . ."

Then the accusations started flying until the whole group

was in an uproar, everyone rushing around shouting, except for David, who retreated to a corner, his eyes never leaving Maude. She was tearing her script, flinging the pieces over the stage with methodical dedication. Wuensche had the look of a defeated general. Bensinger's arms were waving in the air like a conductor's; his big mouth opened and closed, emitting garbled protests.

On an impulse, I scrambled over to Juliet's bureau, pulled out the drawers, and climbed up—no easy task, as the makeshift steps teetered under my weight. No one noticed; they were too busy arguing. Once on top, I crouched down and began barking and howling at the top of my lungs like a dog. For a moment there was shocked silence.

"What's Jodie up to?" Bensinger gasped—furious, indignant. "Come down from there." But I only barked louder. Pouncing around on the rickety chest, I snickered, yapped, and growled at Bensinger. That couldn't go on forever, so I trumpeted like an elephant, burst into a wolf howl. I whinnied, neighed, and cackled until my voice wore out. In short, I went berserk. The whole act took about sixty seconds. Flapping my arms and crowing, I did a rooster imitation, rose and hurled myself off the mahogany ledge, then scampered across the floor, quickly slid under Juliet's bed, and wedged myself into the narrow opening between the dusty floor and bedsprings. Maude leaped up after I poked her in the ankle.

The kids surrounded the bed. "What do you think you're doing?" The angry voices sounded muffled. I lay there silent amid the dust and held back a sneeze. Not so bad in this position, but hardly comfortable. It was a tight squeeze, but I felt snug and safe in the darkness. I waited for a reaction.

"Come out from under there," spluttered Bensinger. His voice sounded like an echo chamber. I refused to budge. For reasons I couldn't explain, once I was jammed under there, I was committed to staying. After all, I would look pretty silly crawling back out. Let them concoct a way to retrieve me. David poked his head down and peered at me, amused.

"I'm stuck," I whispered, trying to sound neutral. The muscles in my neck hurt. I started to feel ridiculous, crammed under there, covered with debris. Up above, the group was having a policy meeting, the chaos of the rehearsal forgotten.

"This will require a major engineering feat," said Bensinger. Shoes scuffled as they circled the bed.

"One, two, three, hike!" And the bed rose into the air as I scuttled backwards like an overturned lobster. David and Mr. Wuensche helped me up, brushing the dust off, laughing.

"What was that all about?" demanded Bensinger.

"All that asinine mucking about," sniffed Maude in her superior tone.

"You look a sight!" from someone else.

"Under the circumstances," I said with cool dignity, "I had to do something." What prompted me was pure panic but it worked—fifteen teenagers were no longer screaming at each other. Instead, they were speechless, looking at me, relieved, shocked, subdued.

"All right, all right," declared Wuensche, "we've had enough for one day. Now that Jodie's provided some comic relief, let's sit down and discuss this problem. As much as it pains me, I have a solution."

Then he made the announcement that should have been made a month earlier. He canceled *Romeo and Juliet*, despite David's feeble protests. Suggesting a student-created production of original skits, he divided us into committees and gave us three weeks to come up with suitable material. Everyone nodded, agreeing to this alternative—everyone but David.

"We tried, but it's no good," concluded Wuensche. "You are a talented group. I know you'll create a show worthy of all our efforts. As Shakespeare once said, 'All's well that ends well.' "

"Hours of work for nothing," David cried in a choking sob. Knocking over a chair, he slammed down his script and rushed out.

I chased after him, but by the time I reached the parking lot, his Jeep was roaring full speed down the road.

16

I WAS actually sitting in a train heading for Grand Central Station. First stop, Stamford. I knew the rest by heart: Old Greenwich, Riverside, Cos Cob, Greenwich, Port Chester, Rye, Harrison, Mamaroneck, and so on. Most things I've learned by rote—$2 \times 2 = 4$, blue and red = purple, the French Revolution 1789–1815—become less important with time, but a few don't. Shakespeare said, "All the world's a stage, / And all the men and women merely players." Timeless, those lines—ones I couldn't forget. Especially that day—when I was acting out a real-life drama. For once I didn't need someone else's script to tell me what to say or do. It was my own drama, mine and David Simms's.

Two days before, he ran away. So upset by the canceled show and a canceled romance, so afraid to face his father, I guess, that he hastily threw his worn clothes in a knapsack and vanished. His family was frantic, but no one knew where he'd gone; no one except me.

"Someday I'll live in New York and spend every day at the Met" kept echoing in my mind. I just knew that was where he was, probably wandering in and out of museums and galleries, trying to find some answers in the world of canvas and paint. I was compelled to search for him. If it hadn't been for my respite with the Simms family, if I had had to endure one more month with Vanessa, it might have been me packing my belongings and running away instead of David. I thought he'd come home, but after two nights I knew he wouldn't.

I was due at the Health Food Store at nine o'clock but found myself running in the other direction, toward the train station, boarding the New Haven Line for New York. There wasn't time to phone Mr. Wheatley. At the time I had only one thought: to find David Simms. Maybe Mr. Wheatley would understand my single-mindedness. It wasn't as if I was a silly, dewy-eyed girl chasing after a boy. David was someone who mattered. It wasn't a rescue mission, either. He was my friend and I sensed what he must have been going through, bogged down with failure. He didn't realize how proud his family was of him and how much his friendship meant to me. Convincing him to return to High Ridge wouldn't be easy. I shouldn't even try, but I could listen. Maybe, as Mr. Wheatley says, "Talking about a problem sometimes makes it better."

There'd never been another opportunity to prove I could be a good friend, even though what I did might have been crazy and impulsive. But impulsive or not, it seemed right.

All my money was wadded up inside the zippered pocket of my ski jacket, $157.67 to be exact, just in case David needed it. I was jittery with excitement.

The train gathered speed. Farmland, subdivisions, factories, rivers, and roads blended into blurred hues. The rectangular window became a screen on which a fast film was projected; my mind played back the series of events that brought me there. Each scene overlapped, collided, raced through my head as quickly as the images outside my window. Nothing was clear except that I was moving forward.

Noon. The light changed. The sun rose above the clouds, flaring in the window, producing a bright glare. For a moment I was engulfed in shadows as the train raced through a tunnel. Light and dark. During the day, shadows and light moved back and forth, playing out a daily drama, shifting, changing, and in the evening, resolution. By dusk, I hoped for a resolution, too.

When the conductor announced, "One Hundred Twenty-fifth Street," I was so eager to begin my search that I ran to the exit door and jumped off the train.

"Where's the Metropolitan Museum?" I asked the first person I saw. A tall, cadaverous man without a coat—strange on this cold day—rubbed his eye with his finger and stared at me blankly. Then he grinned, exposing a mouthful of black, jagged teeth.

"Dontcha want me to show you the way, kiddo?"

I jumped, babbled a high-speed "No indeedy," and hurried off in the direction of the nearest crowd.

"Only old ladies go to the museum," he cackled behind me.

Two chocolate-smeared urchins ran down the stairs to the subway. I followed them on a whim, bought a token, and pushed through the turnstile.

"If you take the express to Eighty-sixth and Lexington, you can walk up to Fifth," a bespectacled woman I judged to be a lawyer told me crisply. Toting a briefcase and an umbrella, she walked away, in very straight, quick, determined steps. I imitated her walk and found I felt thinner and taller.

Once on Fifth Avenue, I was conscious of the high, elegant buildings, the wide avenue, and the streams of well-dressed women who passed me by. Some wore shiny, ankle-length minks, walking tiny, jewel-collared dogs or carrying boxes that proclaimed minor but expensive purchases. Everyone in town seemed to be Christmas shopping. On my left two women rustled by wearing bulbous, down-filled coats of magenta and egg-yolk yellow. Two tiny, bobbing heads emerged above two large plastic bubbles. At their feet were two yipping poodles. As they crossed Eighty-fifth or Eighty-fourth, paused to greet a friend, or used their pooper-scoopers, they discussed their boyfriends. I heard snatches of conversation as I headed for the Met, where I hoped to find David. I've never had a real boy-friend, so I was curious. Maybe some gem would sparkle forth from their ruby lips, some "word from the wise" that I could pass on to David.

"He did this to me and I said . . ."

"You don't need to take that."

"Then I hung up and he called back."

They pecked and pecked, feeding each other tiny worms of information, reminding me of Vanessa and Myrna complaining and commiserating about men. I wondered why men and women find it difficult to get along. Do they expect to feel like Romeo and Juliet all the time? Was that David's problem with Maude? I was being swept down sidewalks, pillowed between goose feathers and fur, feeling like a brussels sprout amid these giant-sized city cabbages.

Roasting chestnuts, a smoky, tangy odor, mingled with the sharp but welcoming smell of hot dogs and mustard. Venders lined the foot of the wide gray staircase above which rose the imposing palace that is called a museum, the repository of High Art, David's Mecca. Ignoring my rumbling stomach, I hopped up the steps two at a time. My hands tightened into two fists pressed against my cheeks. Where else would he be if I don't find him here? Yet once through the revolving door, I realized what an enormous mausoleum this was and how great the odds against finding David were. So many sections and exhibits, too many choices. The posters announced "Costumes of China" in the basement; "Lehman Collection"; the New American Wing, a "Hans Hofmann Show." Hans Hofmann: the name sounded familiar but I couldn't place it.

Trudging upstairs toward the American wing, I clipped the little red admission button on my collar and wondered what I was doing in this place. Made uneasy by all the eager museum-goers shuffling by, I felt a sharp pain in the back of my neck. I was afraid that I wouldn't find David, and I was afraid that I would find him. Not finding him would make this trip useless, but if I did, what would I say? Maybe he'd tell me to go away and leave him alone.

In the first room were floor-to-ceiling portraits of French and English noblemen in plumes and velvet. Patronizingly, they peered at me from their larger-than-life perches on the wall.

In the next room I paused, my face two inches from a juicy portrait of a plump but beautiful young girl holding a cat. I was so intrigued by the patches of muted pastel color, I didn't even turn when someone said, "Watch out, or your nose will scrape the canvas."

"The artist, Renoir, was just here a minute ago," came the voice again. "I told him this picture reminded me of you."

Swinging around and swaying a little, I was face to face

with David Simms, whose mouth crinkled into a smile as he leaned with crossed arms against the white wall.

"Not only the rounded face and blue eyes, but also her dreamy look."

After glancing at the painting again, I decided to take that as a compliment. There were a hundred questions and replies to give him, but I couldn't quite begin. He was surprisingly self-contained, standing there watching me with an almost too alert expression. I expected him to be in a state of wretchedness, but here he was calm, faintly amused, and not even surprised to see me. Maybe this wasn't really David Simms but a museum mirage, a phantasm, a spirit set loose from a painting. I blinked rapidly, but he remained before me.

"I guess you've run into Rembrandt, Picasso, and Van Gogh, too?" I finally said. I expected him to ask what in the world I was doing there, so I hesitated when he motioned me to follow him instead.

"Wait till you see the Hans Hofmann room."

Then I remembered the name; he was one of David's favorite painters.

"You wouldn't think these two colors would look right together," he remarked, pointing to a five-foot-square canvas. Large blocks of pea green and chrome red against a background of pale pink, gray, and off-white. The cubes pushed and pulled off the wall. "A real masterpiece," exclaimed David. To think I used to call a bagel sandwich a masterpiece.

"What's the white remind you of? Egg shells? Clouds? Angora cats? Mashed potatoes? Wonder Bread? Vanilla ice cream? There's a definite structure to this painting. People's eyes are uncoordinated if all they see is a jumble of odd colors. I roam in and out of rooms filled with antique tables and chairs, eighteenth-century landscapes, Dutch still-lifes, ancient carvings, and marble statuary; yet I always end up in front of this Hofmann and the Jackson Pollack drip painting over there. I want to do a painting wide as this whole building and spread it out on the grass in Central Park so children can trample it with bare feet, drop bottle caps and bits of paper on it, so hoboes can rub their cigars out . . ." He was rambling on, gesturing wildly with his hands. Then I noticed his clothes were rumpled. There were dark circles under his eyes. I wondered where he'd slept the last two nights.

"Guess where I've been living?" David's voice had a "proud of myself, bad boy" lilt.

"On a park bench? The Y? The Salvation Army? The gutter?"

He shook his head.

"A sleazy hotel in the Bowery? I know! One of those ladies wrapped in mink with a yapping toy poodle has taken you in."

"Do you ever remember reading a book called *From the Mixed-up Files of Mrs. Basil E. Frankweiler*?"

"Sure . . . this girl and her brother run away from home and hide in the Metropolitan Museum. Did you find the antique bed they used?"

Lowering his voice theatrically, David said, "Let us leave the Hofmanns and I'll show you."

Soon we were in a roped-off cubicle containing an ornate sixteenth-century English bed, enormous and fussy.

"Nothing but the best," I told him.

"I was getting used to all this luxury," remarked David

loudly. Two scholarly types with notebooks gasped when David patted the pillows. A guard called out from across the hall. The whole scene made me laugh especially because I felt implicated, a part of the conspiracy.

"I know you're making this up," I whispered. "Where did you really sleep?"

"At the Port Authority," he admitted. "On the most uncomfortable bench. And my wallet was ripped off, so now I'm broke."

Without even hesitating, I handed him my wad of money. Shaking his head, David said, "No, you keep it. But I'll admit I'm starving. There's homemade soup at a coffee shop down the street. Saw the sign my first day here."

Tactfully I suggested we have some lunch. "I'm hungry, too." The truth was that I was so keyed up, marveling that David Simms had materialized, that food seemed super-fluous, like eating a second dessert.

All the way past the crowded galleries and down the marble staircase, while David held forth about art, a play took place in my mind. I pictured his white Central Park canvas spread across a stage. Various characters—a boy with a dog, a policeman, a nanny wheeling a pram—interact, adding bits and pieces to the canvas. A mosaic recording their individual stories is formed. At the end of the scene the completed canvas is lifted to face the audience. The scenery has been constructed while the play takes place.

I heard David say, "I'm beginning to believe the whole world is a subject for art."

17

"THERE are only a handful of geniuses who rewrite history," remarked David, between large slurps of beef barley soup, "Freud, Einstein, Picasso, Marx. The rest of us muddle along doing the best we can with our meager talents."

"So you think you're a meager talent?" I asked in a half-serious tone. We were sitting in the glassed-in annex of the Madison Grill. I poked at my cottage cheese and tomatoes. David ordered a five-course meal: soup, a BLT sandwich, french fries, salad, and blueberry cobbler. Observing him eat with such relish didn't make me hungry, only curious. Clearly, this was his first meal today.

"I used to think I could change the world," David mused, "that I could do anything; but now . . ." His voice cracked, and fiddling with his fork, he stared distractedly out the window.

"Now what?" Please talk to me was the message I sent him by mental telepathy.

His eyes shifted back to me and his face contorted in a wince of pain. "Now I figure, what's the use?"

I decided not to give him a speech about how wonderful

he was. That would only make him feel worse. I remembered Mr. Wheatley's dictum and decided the best thing to do was coax him to talk.

"Because of the play?" I asked.

"Working on that play, I felt as if I was in the center of a storm all the time. Bensinger baiting me, Wuensche constantly harping on us, changing things, and Maude . . . poor Maude."

"She really gave you a hard time, didn't she?"

"Before I left High Ridge, I went next door and found her perched on a rock, her hair cascading down her back. She was wrapped in a thick green blanket. From the back, Maude reminded me of a mermaid."

I could picture her there like some mythical creature. To David's eyes she must have been dazzling. To me she would have looked like a slimy lizard. "What did she say?"

He laughed hoarsely. "When she finished telling me off, my mind felt empty as if the insides had been scooped out— like a baked potato—and all that was left was the skin." Keep asking leading questions, I told myself. Don't make any nasty cracks about Maude. For once I was determined not to blurt out a remark that might discourage David from talking.

"Is that when you decided to take off?"

"I guess I wasn't thinking clearly. My father doesn't like losers. He would have lectured me about not finishing what I started, even though he never knew what was going on. Mother would pretend that everything was fine, and Heather would say, 'I told you so.' I couldn't face them." I looked at his stricken face, the high ridge of his cheekbones, the dark hollows of his eyes, amazed that he could underestimate his family so much.

"You aren't giving them much credit," I told him, shaking my head in wonder. If you lived with Vanessa, I wanted to say, you'd really find out what a miserable, unsympathetic parent is like.

"Maybe not," he said, "but ever since I was a little kid, first learning to draw, my father has told me, 'If you do something, learn to do it well.' I couldn't even mess up a finger painting without feeling guilty. I remember I'd keep going over and over the paper until the colors were so muddy and wet that I'd have to throw the picture away. Then I'd start over again. 'Is this good?' I'd keep asking Dad. He always said yes, but I never believed what I did was good enough."

"That's because you're too hard on yourself." I was leaning toward him insistently.

"'Just do the best you can, son,'" mimicked David. "That's one expression I'd like to cross off Dad's list." I wasn't used to David making negative remarks about his father; but his voice didn't sound very convincing. He fingered his french fries, and I realized he was homesick, trying to find excuses for not going back.

"Vanessa never said 'good' to anything I ever did. How would you like to live like that?" My sympathetic mothering instincts had vanished, my calmness was shattered.

"You're lucky," I said harshly, the tears welling in my eyes, "and you don't even realize it."

David Simms could return to his beautiful house in the country and his family, who would welcome him home with a brass band and a parade if need be. What did I have to go back for? Just the thought of Vanessa triggered the familiar gnawing in my stomach, but I didn't need to eat. I had discovered that whenever I felt nervous now, instead of going on a food binge, I could let it pass. Eventually the tugging sensation went away.

Cocking his head to one side, David eyed me, surprised by my outburst. Neither of us spoke for a while.

Finally he said, "The truth is, I was relieved when Mr. Wuensche canned the play. I just couldn't admit it."

"I know," I said, helping myself to a bite of his dessert. "But that doesn't mean you failed."

David chewed on his sandwich thoughtfully. To release pent-up tension, he pounded on the bottom of the Heinz bottle. Catsup splattered the table, just missing his plate.

"Try again." I giggled. He offered me a soggy french fry. Wolfing down the blueberry cobbler, he wiped his mouth with a napkin and started grinning.

When the waitress handed him the check, David said, "I guess I'll have to go back and wash dishes."

For a moment, the waitress looked surprised. Then she smiled.

"Consider this meal my treat," I insisted, pulling a wrinkled bill out of my pocket. Suddenly lighthearted, I felt daring, as if I'd just ridden over the crest of a high wave and was cruising in to shore.

Linking arms, we traversed the long sidewalk, ducked around the down-coated ladies rolling along Madison, and dashed back to the Met. We became fast-paced New Yorkers, spurred on by renewed energy, a sense of adventure. We broke hands when an especially purposeful shopper bore down on us, her eyes glinting, her Gucci bag swinging. In the streets, cabs honked, splattering the slush. The air was heavy with grime.

"I need the clean smell of the woods," David said. "I can't face another day in this city." A good sign, I thought.

As we wandered around looking at Christmas decorations, I mentioned David's happening in Central Park, how it might work as a theater piece. He listened but didn't respond. Soon we had walked in three circles around Bloomingdale's and I was freezing. David stuffed his hands in his pockets. Our pace had slowed to a shuffle. We loitered in front of a florist shop. The window displayed a perfect old-fashioned country Christmas. An antique oak table was set with white stoneware on green and red patchwork mats, with a centerpiece of holly and poinsettia in a copper pot. Old woolen embroidered stockings filled with candy canes hung next to a wood-burning stove. David made a wry face.

I tugged on his sleeve. "Hey, why don't we go home?"

Without answering, he took off down the block. Instead of chasing after him, I took my time. When I turned the corner, he was waiting. He smiled and cupped my chin in his hand. This time I wasn't afraid to look him in the eye.

"Jodie, your idea for Wuensche's new wonder might work. Let's plan it together on the train back to High Ridge." Unable to contain myself, I let out a loud cheer. When he threw his arms around me, I didn't pull away.

"And by the way," he added mischievously, "you'll have to re-enact the barking episode on top of the bureau. That was a classic."

18

"Do you think there will be trumpets heralding our return to High Ridge?" I remarked to David when the train finally pulled into the depot.

"We'll be our own welcoming committee," he answered, surveying the streets, which were almost deserted at this late hour.

The train headed off toward New Haven; a cat whined in the alley; the melancholy tune on a juke box wailed from the corner tavern; a jalopy full of rowdy kids cruised down Main Street. Yet the familiar billboards and dilapidated buildings gave me a surprising sense of security, as if New York with all its frenetic allure was very far away. High Ridge had undergone no major transformation, but my perceptions had altered. In the interval between two train rides, the town became my central focus—a skit to prepare with David, my job at Mr. Wheatley's. I tried not to think about my reunion with Vanessa.

Arm in arm, David and I progressed along the back streets toward his house. After an hour of non-stop talking, sharing confidences on the train, we lapsed into comfortable silence. Ice packed the sidewalk. I slid across slippery paths as if gliding on imaginary skates. My feet touched ground but I felt weightless, floating past snow-laden pines, white houses, and frozen ponds. The moon cast a fairy-tale glow over the sleeping neighborhood.

At the Simmses', lights blazed from every window; his parents were keeping vigil. David hesitated at the gate; his hand trembled when he unlatched the lock.

"Why don't I sneak up the back stairs," I suggested, "so you can meet your family in private?" Also, I wanted to phone Mr. Wheatley to explain why I didn't show up for work. Before I had a chance to slip past the front door, it swung open and out dashed Heather, followed by Mr. and Mrs. Simms, the cat—and Vanessa Firestone herself! There was a round of embracing, crying, and playful rough-housing, in the midst of which I was enfolded. A free-for-all! Hugs were exchanged, everyone shouting at the same time. I had emerged the heroine. Not given to joyful outbursts, Vanessa halted at the landing and regarded me non-committally.

It was strange but until that moment I'd always felt so dependent on the Simmses, as if I'd been taken in and nurtured like a stray cat. They seemed so perfect, a family with everything, and that separated us no matter how wonderful they were to me. But even in perfect families, things can go wrong. By bringing David home, I'd been able to help them. They had needed me, and somehow I felt the gap that stretched between us was closing.

"Jodie, you're terrific," said Mr. Simms.

"The best," added Heather. I felt great. I hoped my mother was listening.

Then Mr. Simms began firing questions at David, demanding an explanation, and what had begun as a celebration turned into a cross-examination. I didn't blame him, but I also didn't want to be in the middle. David could work things out with his family by himself. I still had my own problems to deal with.

I disentangled myself from the family and turned to Vanessa, who was holding the cat. Plato licked her sun-tanned cheeks. Dressed in a wild flowered affair, Vanessa stood there with seashells dangling from her ears and tears in her eyes. I expected Vanessa to be screaming, not crying for me.

"I was worried, Jodie. Myrna and I decided to come back early. But when I called to tell you to come home, Mr. Simms said you'd disappeared. I rushed over and have been sitting here with the Simmses, trying to figure out what to do next." She paused. "They've been very nice." I knew it took an effort for her to admit that, but what could I say?

Then she was tugging my arm, leading me out of the cold. "I'm proud of you. Now that we're both back, let's go home." I stared at her, amazed. What did she mean, "proud of me"? True, I'd lost some weight, but I was hardly bony. What was she so proud about? Reuniting the Simms family could hardly thrill my mother, who'd always regarded them with the friendliness of a porcupine.

I stiffened and shrugged her hand off my arm. I wasn't sure I wanted to go with her. What did I have to go back to? A dingy room and a nagging mother. Yet I sensed a change in her. She looked small, not the looming hawk-like figure I imagined when she wasn't around. Or maybe I was the one who had changed.

In a resigned voice she said, "I can see what you find so appealing here. I'm going back to the apartment, but you can stay as long as you like."

Traipsing into the house, the Simmses headed for the kitchen. Mr. Simms's arm was thrown over David's shoulder, which meant they'd straightened things out. I smelled hot chocolate. Strangely, I didn't want my mother to leave, but how could I tell her?

Finally I made a feeble remark. "You've really got a good tan." At least I kept the conversation going. Comments about Vanessa's looks usually brought a response from her.

"You won't believe this, but all that sun and sea air made me feel so healthy, I actually forgot to worry about how I looked. Maybe I've made too big a deal out of it." Then she paused. "You look better, too."

I decided to take the bull by the horns. "But what if you found me still as fat as ever? You'd probably be having a fit." If only I felt warmth toward her instead of suspicion.

"Jodie, you're not making this very easy for me." She lit a cigarette and began her familiar pacing.

I knew I was giving her a hard time. I didn't want to be mean, but I was afraid that any concession, even a small one, would be like submitting totally. Thoughts I had held back came pouring out in a rush of half-sentences and garbled phrases. "I can't do it your way . . . never . . . not like you. I don't want to be compared . . . don't. I can't, not any more." I could hear my own voice rising as the noise level in the kitchen dropped. How I wished I were in there sipping cocoa, this confrontation with Vanessa over.

She looked back self-consciously. "I know. I know," she whispered as if lowering her voice would lower mine. "Can't we talk about this at home?" As I stared at my mother, I knew I could never be the person she invented for me. If I couldn't totally please her, then I had to learn to please myself. In her own way Vanessa loved me, and that had to be enough, at least for now. But if we were ever to straighten things out between us, I needed to go home.

"Will you wait while I pack my suitcase?"

She moved toward me and placed her hand on mine, but again I stiffened. I just wasn't used to her touching me. I told each muscle to relax. What made me so jumpy? She was making an effort, and there was nothing phony about it. Yet some instinct prevented me from grasping her hand. Afraid to say or do the wrong thing, I was groping my way through a labyrinth of words and one wrong move, one wrong word, would either put us back where we started or leave us stuck, with no way out.

"It will be all right," she said as much to herself as to me.

"I'll be right back," I muttered, running upstairs to the safety of the guest room. There, on the patchwork quilt, I sat and tried to sort out my feelings. I dreaded going back to my dreary room. Seeing that musty old apartment would be proof that nothing had changed. As I packed my clothes, I realized how much I loved sleeping in the canopy bed, how much I had enjoyed every object in that room, from the Currier and Ives prints to the faded Persian rug. The old highboy, the roll-top walnut desk, the Meissen lamp: each piece was carefully placed, beautiful and old-fashioned. The Simmses' possessions represented them perfectly. I didn't want to live in a drab, ugly bedroom any more. I didn't want to go back to being picked on by Vanessa. But situations don't have to stay the same. There was no reason why I couldn't change my bedroom, redo the whole thing. And if I could make changes, I had to trust that Vanessa could change, too. Maybe we both could.

At that moment, Heather and David burst in. David's wary, anxious look had faded. I hoped he was finally over Maude St. James, but I knew it would take a while.

"I'll miss you," I said, "but I have to leave now."

"I hate goodbyes," Heather moaned. "Maybe we'll adopt your mother so you can stay. Oh yes—Mr. Wheatley called. I told him what happened and he said the oddest thing. 'Jodie will find what she's after,' he told me, 'and it won't be a hot fudge sundae.'"

"It's a long story, but I knew he'd understand." I hugged Heather.

"Don't forget about me," David said, hiking my suitcase over his shoulder. "We have a project to do together." "Thank you" he mouthed in back of his sister. I wondered if that day would mark a beginning, if I'd remember it later as a turning point for David, for me, and for my mother. I had moved forward on the train that morning. I was still moving forward.

After receiving a bear hug from Mr. Simms and a peck on the cheek from Mrs. Simms, Vanessa and I descended into the snowy dark. Together we scraped the ice from the windshield.

"I've decided to use my earnings to redecorate my room," I told Mother when we settled into the car. She handed me a bulky package. Ripping the brown wrapping, I found a bright yellow handwoven spread inside.

"An early Christmas present," she said. It was the first present she'd ever given me that wasn't a reward for losing weight or getting a good grade.

As we sat in the dark, enclosed together, large, wet snowflakes fell on the windows. Tears fell down my cheeks. I wanted to accept the present and believe the bad feelings between us would fade away, that my mother and I would get along, that somehow I could please her. But I knew that I had to keep a part of myself separate, that I had to be myself. That realization allowed me to take her hand. It had an unfamiliar softness. I held on, getting used to the new sensation.

"I love the spread. It will be perfect for my room. Thank you." She squeezed my hand and started the motor.

"Now, if I were you," Mother said, "I'd do the whole bedroom in vivid colors."

"But I'm not you," I said quietly.

She nodded. Out of the wall that was between us came one brick at a time.